The Pony Rider Boys In The Grand Canyon

or

The Mystery Of Bright Angel Gulch

Frank Gee Patchin

The Pony Rider Boys in The Grand Canyon

Frank Gee Patchin

PO Box 2211
Fairfield, IA 52556
www.1stworldlibrary.org
First Edition

LCCN: 2004195616

Softcover ISBN: 1-4218-0437-9
Hardcover ISBN: 1-4218-0337-2
eBook ISBN: 1-4218-0537-5

The Pony Rider Boys in The Grand Canyon

contributed by Tim, Ed & Rodney

in support of

1st World Library Literary Society

CONTENTS

CHAPTER I

WESTWARD HO!

"Ow, Wow, Wow, Wow! Y-E-O-W!"

Tad Butler, who was industriously chopping wood at the rear of the woodshed of his home, finished the tough, knotted stick before looking up.

The almost unearthly chorus of yells behind him had not even startled the boy or caused him to cease his efforts until he had completed what he had set out to do. This finished, Tad turned a smiling face to the three brown-faced young men who were regarding him solemnly.

"Haven't you fellows anything to do?" demanded Tad.

"Yes, but we have graduated from the woodpile," replied Ned Rector.

"I got my diploma the first time I ever tried it," added Chunky Brown, otherwise and more properly known as Stacy Brown. "Cut a slice of my big toe off. They gave me my diploma right away. You fellows are too slow."

"Come in the house, won't you? Mother'll be glad to

see you," urged Tad.

"Surely we will," agreed Walter Perkins. "That's what we came over to do."

"Oh, it is, eh?"

"Didn't think we came over to help you chop wood, did you?" demanded Chunky indignantly.

"Knowing you as I do, I hadn't any such idea," laughed Tad."But come in."

The boys filed in through the wood house, reaching the sitting room by way of the kitchen. Tad's mother gave them a smiling welcome, rising to extend a warm, friendly hand to each.

"Sit down, Mrs.Butler," urged Walter.

"Yes, we will come to you," added Ned.

"We haven't lost the use of our legs yet, Mrs.Butler," declared the fat Chunky, growing very red in the face as he noted the disapproving glances directed at him by his companions.

"I hope you won't mind Chunky, Mrs.Butler," said Ned apologetically."You know he has lived among savages lately, and --- "

"Yes, ma'am, Ned and I have been constant companions for -- how long has it been, boys?"

"Shut up!" hissed Ned Rector in the fat boy's ear. "I'll whale you when we get outside, if you make any more such breaks."

"Never mind, boys; Stacy and myself are very old, old friends," laughed Mrs.Butler.

"Yes, ma'am, about a hundred years old, more or less. Oh, I beg your pardon. I didn't mean it just that way," stammered Chunky, coloring
again and fumbling his cap awkwardly.

"Now you have said it," groaned Walter.

"Go way back in the corner out of sight and sit down before I start something," commanded Ned."You must excuse us, Mrs.Butler. It is as Chunky has said.We are all savages -- some of us more so than others, some less."

"It is unnecessary to make apologies.You are just a lot of healthy young men, full of life and spirits." Mrs.Butler patted Tad affectionately on the head. "Tad knows what I think of you all and how appreciative we both are over what Mr.Perkins has done for us.Now that I have had a little money left me, I am glad that Tad is able to spend more time with you in the open. I presume you will soon be thinking of another trip."

"We're always thinking of that, Mrs.Butler," interrupted Ned. "And we couldn't think of a trip without thinking of Tad. A trip without Tad would be like -- like --- "

"A dog's tail wagging down the street without the dog," interjected the solemn voice of Chunky Brown from his new headquarters.

"I move we throw Chunky out in the wood house," exploded Ned. "Will you excuse us while we get rid of the encumbrance, Mrs.Butler?"

"Sit down and make your peace. I know you boys have some things to talk over. I can see it in your faces. Go on with your conference. I'll bring you some lemonade in a few moments," said Mrs.Butler, as she left the room.

"Well, fellows, is this just a friendly call or have you really something in mind?" asked Tad after all had seated themselves.

"I'm the only one with a mind that will hold anything. And I've got plenty in it, too," piped Chunky.

Ned Rector sighed helplessly. The other boys grinned, passing hands across their faces that Stacy might not observe their amusement.

"We want to pow-wow with you," said Walter.

"That means you've something ahead -- another trip?"

"Yes, we're going to the --- " began young Brown.

"Silence! Children should be seen, but not heard," commanded Ned.

Chunky promptly hitched his chair out, joining the circle.

"I'm seen," he nodded, with a grimace.

"Then see that you're not heard. Some things not even

a Pony Rider boy can stand. You're one of them."

"Yes, I'm a Pony Rider," answered Chunky, misapplying Ned Rector's withering remark.

"Another trip, eh?"

"That's it, Tad. Walt's father has planned it out for us. And what do you think?"

"Yes, what d'ye think? He's going --- "

"Look here, Chunky, are you telling this or am I?" demanded Ned angrily.

"You're trying to, but you're making an awful mess of the whole business. Better let me tell it. I know how and you don't."

"Give Ned a chance, can't you, Chunky?" rebuked Tad, frowning.

"All right, I'll give him a chance, of course, if you say so. I always have to take a back seat for everybody. I'm nothing but just a roly-poly fat boy, handy to draw water, pitch and strike camp, gather firewood, wash the dishes, cook the meals, save the lives of my companions when they get into scrapes, and --- "

This was too much for the gravity of the Pony Rider Boys. They burst out into a hearty laugh, which served to put all in good humor again. Chunky, having relieved his mind, now settled down in his chair to listen.

"Now, Ned, proceed," said Tad.

"Well, Mr.Perkins thinks it would be fine for us to visit the Grand Canyon."

"Of the Colorado?"

"Yes."

"Tad knows more'n the rest of you. You didn't know where the place was.Walt thought it was some kind of a gun that they shot off at sunrise, or --- "

No one gave any heed to Chunky's further interruption this time.

"The Grand Canyon of the Colorado?" repeated Tad, his eyes sparkling. "Isn't that fine? Do you know, I have always wanted to go there, but I hardly thought we should get that far away from home again. But what plans has Mr.Perkins made?"

"Well, he has been writing to arrange for guides and so forth. He knows a good man at Flagstaff with whom Mr.Perkins hunted a few years ago. What did he say the name was, Walt?"

"Nance. Jim Nance, one of the best men in that part of the country. Everybody knows Jim Nance."

"I don't," declared Chunky, suddenly coming to life again.

"There are a lot of other things you don't know," retorted Ned Rector witheringly.

"If there are you can't teach them to me," returned Stacy promptly.

"As I was saying when *that* interrupted me, Mr.Perkins wrote to this man, Nance, and engaged him for June first, to remain with us as long as we require his services."

"Does Mr.Perkins think we had better take our ponies with us?"

"No."

"Then we shall have to buy others. I hardly think I can afford that outlay," said Tad, with a shake of the head.

"That is all arranged, Tad," interrupted Walter. "Father has directed Mr.Nance to get five good horses or ponies."

"Then Professor Zepplin is to accompany us?"

"Yes."

"Poor Professor! His troubles certainly are not over yet," laughed Tad. "We must try not to annoy him so much this trip. We are older now and ought to use better judgment."

"That's what I've been telling Ned," spoke up Stacy. "He's old enough to --- "

"To -- what?" demanded Ned.

Chunky quailed under the threatening gaze of Ned Rector. He mumbled some unintelligible words, settled back in his chair and made himself as inconspicuous as possible.

"Pooh! Professor Zepplin enjoys our pranks as much as do we ourselves. He just makes believe that he doesn't. He's a boy himself."

"But an overgrown one," muttered Stacy under his breath.

"Where do we meet the Professor?" asked Tad.

"How about it, Walt?" asked Ned, turning to young Perkins.

"I don't think father mentioned that."

"We shall probably pick him up on the way out," nodded Tad.

"Well, what do you think of it?" demanded Ned.

"Fine, fine!"

"You don't seem very enthusiastic about it."

"Don't I? Well, I am. Has Mr.Perkins decided when we are to start?"

"Yes, in about two weeks."

"I don't know. I am afraid that is too soon for me. I don't even know that I shall be able to go," said Tad Butler.

"Why not?"

"Well, we may not be able to afford it."

"Pshaw! Your mother just said you might go, or words to that effect. Of course you'll go. If you didn't, I wouldn't go, and my father would be disappointed. He knows what these trips have done for me. Remember what a tender plant I was when we went out in the Rockies that time?"

"Ye -- yes," piped Stacy. "He was a pale lily of the valley. Now Walt's a regular daisy."

Young Perkins laughed good-naturedly. He was not easily irritated now, whereas, before beginning to live in the open, the least little annoyance would set his nerves on edge.

Mrs.Butler came in at this juncture, carrying a pitcher of lemonade and four glasses on a tray. The Pony Riders rose instinctively, standing while Mrs.Butler poured the lemonade.

"Oh, I forgot the cookies, didn't I?" she cried.

"Yes, we couldn't get along without the cookies," nodded Chunky.

"Now don't let your eyes get bigger'n your stomach," warned Ned. "Remember, we are in polite society now."

"I hope you won't forget yourself either," retorted Stacy. "I'll stand beside you. If you start to make a break I'll tread on your toes and --- "

"Try it!" hissed Ned Rector in the fat boy's ear. The entrance of Mrs.Butler with a plate heaped with ginger cookies drove all other thoughts from the minds of the boys. "Mrs.Butler," began Ned, clearing his throat, "we -- we thank you; from the bottom of our hearts we thank you -- don't we, Stacy?"

"Well, I -- I guess so. I can tell better after I've tried the cookies. I know the lemonade's all right."

"How do you know?" demanded three voices at once.

"Why, I tasted of it," admitted Chunky.

"As I was saying, Mrs.Butler, we --- "

"Never mind thanking me, Ned. I will take your appreciation for granted."

"Thank you," answered Stacy, looking longingly at the plate of cookies.

"Now help yourselves. Don't wait, boys," urged Tad's mother, giving the boys a friendly smile before turning to leave the room.

"Ah, Mrs.Butler. One moment, please," said Ned.

"Yes. What is it?"

"We -- ah --- "

"Oh, let me say it. You don't know how to talk in public," exclaimed Chunky. "Mrs.Butler, we, the Pony Rider Boys, rough riders, Indian fighters and general, all-around stars of both plain and mountain, are thinking --- "

Ned thrust Chunky gently aside. Had it not been for

Mrs.Butler's presence Ned undoubtedly would have used more force.

Tad sat down grinning broadly. He knew that his mother enjoyed this good-natured badinage fully as much as the boys did.

Ned rapped on the table with his knuckles.

"Order, please, gentlemen!"

"That's I," chuckled Stacy, slipping into a chair.

"Laying all trimmings aside, Mrs.Butler, we have come to speak with you first, after which we'll have something to say to your son."

Mrs.Butler sat down in the chair that Tad had placed for her.

"Very good. I shall be glad to hear what you have to say, Ned."

"The fact is -- as I was about to say when interrupted by the irresponsible person at my left --- "

"I beg pardon. *I'm* at your left," remarked Walter.

"He doesn't know which is his left and which is his right," jeered Chunky. "He's usually left, though."

"I refer to the person who was sitting at my left at the time I began speaking. I had no intention of casting any aspersion on Mr.Walter Perkins. As I was about to say, we are planning another trip, Mrs. Butler."

"Where away this time, Ned?"

"To the Grand Canyon --- "

"With the accent on the *yon*," added Stacy.

"The Grand Canyon of the Colorado?"

"Yes, ma'am. Mr.Perkins has arranged it for us. Everything is fixed. Professor Zepplin is going along and --- "

"That will be fine, indeed," glowed Tad's mother.

"Yes, we think so, and we're glad to know that you do. Tad didn't know whether you would approve of the proposed trip or not. We are -- ahem -- delighted to learn that you do approve of it and that you are willing that Tad should go."

"Oh, but I haven't said so," laughed Mrs.Butler.

"Of course she hasn't. You see how little one can depend upon what Ned Rector says," interjected Stacy.

Ned gave him a warning look.

"I should say that you approve of his going. Of course we couldn't think of taking this trip without Tad. I don't believe Mr.Perkins would let Walt go if Tad weren't along. You see, Tad's a handy man to have around. I know Chunky's people never would trust him to go without Tad to look after him. You see, Chunky's such an irresponsible mortal --- "

"Oh, I don't know," interrupted the fat boy.

"One never knows what he's going to do next. He needs some one to watch him constantly. We think it is the fault of his bringing up."

"Or the company I've been keeping," finished Chunky.

"At any rate, we need Tad with us."

"Then I shall have to say 'yes,'" replied Mrs.Butler, nodding and smiling. "Of course Tad may go. I am glad, indeed, that he has such splendid opportunities."

"But, mother, I ought to be at work," protested Tad. "It is time I were doing something. Besides, I think you need me at home."

"Never mind, Tad. When you have finished with these trips you will be all the better for them. You will have erected a foundation of health that will last you all your life. Furthermore, you will have gained many things by the experience, When you get at the real serious purpose of your life, you will accomplish what you set yourself to do, with better results."

"That -- that's what I say," began Chunky. "Haven't I always told you --- "

"Stacy is wise beyond his years," smiled Mrs.Butler. "When he is grown up I look for him to be a very clever young man."

The eyes of the boys still twinkled merrily, for Chunky, unable to guess whether he were being teased, was still scowling somewhat. However, he kept still for the time being.

"Yes, Tad may go with you," continued Mrs.Butler. "You start -- when?"

"In about two weeks," Walter replied. "Father said he would call to discuss the matter with you."

"I shall be glad of that," nodded Mrs.Butler. "I shall want to talk over the business part of the trip."

Then the youngsters fell to discussing the articles of outfit they would need. On this head their past experience stood them in good stead.

"Now, I presume, I have said all that I can say," added Mrs.Butler, rising. "I will leave you, for I would be of very little use to you in choosing clothing and equipment."

Before she could escape from the room, however, Tad had risen and reached her. Without exhibiting a twinge of embarrassment before the other young men, Tad held and kissed her, then escorted her to the door. Walter and Ned smiled their approval. Chunky said nothing, but sat blinking solemnly -- the best possible proof of his approbation.

All of the readers of this series know these young men well. They were first introduced to Tad and his chums in the opening volume, "*The Pony Rider Boys In The Rockies*." Then were told all the details of how the boys became Pony Riders, and of the way they put their plans through successfully. Readers of that volume well recall the exciting experiences and hair-breadth escapes of the youngsters, their hunts for big game and all the joys of living close to Nature. Their battle with the claim jumpers is still fresh in the minds of all readers.

We next met our young friends in the second volume, "*The Pony Rider Boys In Texas.*" It was on these south-western grazing plains that the lads took part in a big cattle drive across the state. This new taste of cowboy life furnished the boys with more excitement than they had ever dreamed could be crowded into so few weeks. It proved to be one long round of joyous life in the saddle, yet it was the sort of joy that is bound up in hard work. Tad's great work in saving a large part of the herd will still be fresh in the mind of the reader. How the lads won the liking of even the roughest cowboys was also stirringly told.

From Texas, as our readers know, the Pony Riders went north, and their next doings are interestingly chronicled in "*The Pony Rider Boys In Montana.*" Here the boys had the great experience of going over the old Custer trail, and here it was that Tad and his companions became involved in a "war" between the sheep and the cattle men. How Tad and his chums soon found themselves almost in the position of the grist between the millstones will be instantly recalled. Tad's adventures with the Blackfeet Indians formed not the least interesting portion of the story. It was a rare picture of ranch and Indian life of the present day that our readers found in the third volume of this series.

Perhaps the strangest experiences, as most of our readers will agree, were those described in "*The Pony Rider Boys In The Ozarks.*" In this wild part of the country the Pony Rider Boys had a medley of adventures -- they met with robbers, were lost in the great mountain forests, and unexpectedly became involved in an accident in a great mine. The final discovery of the strange secret of the mountains was the climax of that wonderful saddle journey.

From the wooded Ozarks to the stifling alkali deserts of Nevada was a long jump, but the lads made it. All of our readers remember the rousing description of adventures that were set forth in "*The Pony Rider Boys In The Alkali*." This trip through the grim desert with its scanty vegetation and scarcity of water proved to be a journey that fully demonstrated the enduring qualities of these sturdy young men. The life, far away from all connection with civilization, was one of constant privation and well-nigh innumerable perils. The meeting with the crazed hermit of this wild waste formed one of the most thrilling incidents. The whole vast alkali plain presented a maze the solving of which taxed to the utmost the ingenuity of the young men. However, they bore themselves with credit, and came out with a greater reputation than ever for judgment, courage and endurance.

Our next meeting with these lads, who were fast becoming veterans of the saddle, was in the sixth volume, "*The Pony Rider Boys in New Mexico*." Here, again, the lads ran upon Indian "signs" and experiences, not the least of which was their chance to be present at the weird fire dance of the Apaches. The race with the prairie fire, the wonderful discoveries made in the former homes of the cave-dwellers, and the defence of the lost treasure in the home of the ancient Pueblo Indians are all matters well remembered by our readers.

Now another journey, to the scene of one of Nature's greatest wonders, the Grand Canyon of the Colorado, was absorbing the thought of Tad Butler and his young friends.

"The question is, what'll we take with us?" asked Ned Rector.

"Yes, that's one of the things about which we wanted to talk with you," spoke up Walter Perkins. "You always think of things that none of the rest of us remembers."

"Oh, I don't know. You're all pretty good planners. In the first place, you know you want to travel light."

"We aren't likely to travel any other way," scoffed Chunky. "Whatever we do, though, let's not travel light on food. I can stand almost anything but food -- I mean without food -- I mean --- "

"I don't believe you know what you do mean," jeered Ned. "Well, what about it, Tad?"

"As I was saying, we should travel light. Of course, we must take our own equipment -- saddles, quirts, spurs, chaps, lasso, guns, canteen, slicker and all that sort of thing. I suppose the guide will arrange for the pack train equipment."

"I'll speak to father about that," said Walter. "I don't know just what arrangements he has made with the guide."

"We can no doubt get what ammunition we need after we get to Flagstaff, if that is to be our railway destination. Folks usually have ammunition in that country," added Tad, with a faint smile. "Our uniforms or clothes we know about. We shall no doubt need some good tough boots for mountain climbing --- "

"Do we have to climb mountains?" demanded Stacy.

"Climb up and fall down," answered Walt.

"Oh, dear me, dear me! It'll be the death of me, I know," wailed the fat boy. "I'd rather ride -- up. I can get down all right, but --- "

"Yes, you certainly can get down," laughed Ned.

"Then we shall want quite a lot of soft, strong rope, about quarter-inch Manila. I don't think of anything else. We ought to be able to pick up whatever else we need after we get out there -- -- "

"I guess that's all, fellows, isn't it?" asked Ned.

"All but the shouting," answered Stacy.

"You are well able to do that. You'd better practise up on those favorite exclamations of yours -- "

"What are they?"

"Y-e-o-w and W-o-w!"

"Who-o-o-p-e-e!" answered Chunky in a shrill, high-pitched voice.

Ned Rector clapped a hand over the fat boy's mouth with a resounding smack. Chunky was jerked backward, his head striking the chair with a bump that was audible all over the room.

"You stop that business. Do you forget where you are? That's all right out in the wilds, but not in civilized society," declared Ned.

"Whe -- where's the civilized society? Don't you do that to me again, or I'll --- "

"Chunky's all right. Let him alone, Ned. Mother doesn't care how much noise we make in here. In fact, she'd think something was wrong with us if we didn't make a big racket. Chunky, if you are so full of steam you might go out and finish the woodpile for me. I've got to cut that wood this afternoon."

"No, thank you. I'm willing to hunt for the colored man in the woodpile, but I'm a goat if I'll chop the wood. Why, I'd lose my reputation in Chillicothe if I were seen doing such a common thing as that."

"No, that would be impossible," answered Ned sarcastically.

"Eh? Impossible?" questioned Stacy.

"Oh, yes, yes, yes. I'll write it down for you so you'll understand it and --- "

"He means that you can't lose what you don't possess," explained Walter.

Chunky grunted his disgust, but made no reply. The boys then fell to discussing the proposed trip. Tad got out his atlas and together they pored over the map of Arizona. After some time at this task, Chunky pulled a much soiled railway map from his pocket. This gave them a more detailed plan of the Grand Canyon.

"You see, I have to show you. When it comes to doing things Stacy Brown's the one on whom you all have to fall back."

"You are almost human at times, Stacy. I'm free to admit that," laughed Tad. "Yes, this is just what we want."

Chunky inflated his chest, and, with hands clasped behind his back, walked to the window and gazed out into the street, nodding patronizingly now and then to persons passing who had bowed to him. In his own estimation, Stacy was the most important person in Chillcothe. So confident was he of this that several persons in the community had come almost to believe it themselves. Chunky, by his dignified and important bearing, had hopes of converting others to this same belief. As for his three companions -- well, a journey without Stacy Brown would be a tame and uneventful journey at best.

The greater part of the afternoon was devoted to making plans for the coming trip, each having his suggestions to make or his criticism to offer of the suggestions of others. Though the arguments of the Pony Riders at times became quite heated, the friendship they held for each other was never really strained. They were bound together by ties that would endure for many years to come.

Each day thereafter, during their stay at home, they met for consultation, and when two weeks later they had assembled at the railroad station in Chillicothe, clad in their khaki suits, sombreros, each with a red bandanna handkerchief tied carelessly about his neck, they presented an imposing appearance and were the centre of a great crowd of admiring boys and smiling grown-ups. There were many exciting experiences ahead of the Pony Rider Boys as well as a series of journeys that would linger in memory the rest of their lives.

CHAPTER II

A VIEW OF THE PROMISED LAND

For nearly three days the Pony Rider Boys had been taking their ease in a Pullman sleeping car, making great inroads on the food served in the dining car.

It had been a happy journey. The boys were full of anticipation of what was before them. At intervals during the day they would study their maps and enter into long discussions with Professor Zepplin, the grizzled, stern-looking man who in so many other journeys had been their guardian and faithful companion. The Professor had joined them at St.Louis, where the real journey had commenced.

All that day they had been racing over baked deserts, a cloud of dust sifting into the car and making life miserable for the more tender passengers, though the hardy Pony Riders gave no heed to such trivial discomforts as heat and dust. They were used to that sort of thing. Furthermore, they expected, ere many more days had passed, to be treated to discomforts that were real.

Suddenly the train dashed from the baked desert into a green forest. The temperature seemed to drop several degrees in an instant. Everyone drew a long breath, faces were pressed against windows and expressions of delight were heard in many parts of the sleeper.

They had entered a forest of tall pines, so tall that the lads were obliged to crane their necks to see the tops.

"This is the beginning of the beginning," announced Professor Zepplin somewhat enigmatically. "This is the forest primeval."

"I don't know," replied Chunky, peering through a car window. "It strikes me that we've left the evil behind and got into the real thing."

"What is it, Professor?" asked Tad Butler.

"As I have said, it is a primeval forest. This great woodland stretches away from the very base of the San Francisco mountains southward for a distance of nearly two hundred miles. We are taking a short cut through it and should reach Flagstaff in about an hour from now."

"Hurrah! We're going to see the Flagstaff in an hour," cried Stacy, his face wreathed in smiles.

"A further fact, which is no doubt unknown to you, is that this enormous forest covers an area of over ten thousand square miles, and contains six million, four hundred thousand acres."

The boys uttered exclamations of amazement and wonder.

"If you'd said ten acres, I'd understand you better," replied Stacy. "I never could think in such big figures. I'm like a rich fellow in our town, who doesn't know what money is above a certain sum."

"Well, what about it?" demanded Tad.

"Up to fifty dollars, he knows how much it is, but for anything above that it's a check," finished Chunky, looking about him expectantly.

No one laughed.

"Speaking of checks," said Ned Rector after an interval of silence, "did you bring along that snaffle bit, Tad?"

"What snaffle bit?"

"The one we were going to put on Stacy Brown to hold him in check?"

A series of groans greeted Ned's words. Chunky grumbled something about making a checker board of Ned's face if he didn't watch out, after which the Professor turned the rising tide into other and safer channels by continuing his lecture on the great Arizona forest.

As the train dashed on the Pony Riders were greeted with occasional views of a mountain differing from anything they ever had seen. One peak especially attracted their attention. Its blackened sides, and its summit bathed in a warm glow of yellow sunshine, gave it a most striking appearance.

"What is it, Professor?" asked Tad, with an inquiring gaze and nod toward the mountain.

"Sunset Mountain," answered Professor Zepplin. "You

should have discovered that."

"But it isn't sunset," objected Walter.

"It is always sunset there. The effect is always a sunset effect."

"In the night, too!" questioned Chunky.

"No, it's moonset then," scoffed Rector.

"In the same direction you will observe the others of the San Francisco mountains. However, we shall have more of this later on. For the present you would do well to gather up Your belongings, for we shall be at our journey's end in a few minutes."

This announcement caused the boys to spring up, reaching to the racks above for such of their luggage as had been stowed there. All was bustle for the next twenty minutes. Then the train drew into the station, the cars covered with the dust of the desert, changing the dark brown of their paint to a dirty gray.

The boys found that they had arrived at a typical western town, a tree-surrounded, mountain-shadowed, breeze-blown place set like a gem in a frame of green and gold, nestling, it seemed, at the very base of the towering peaks of the San Francisco mountains, whose three rough volcanic peaks stood silent sentinel over the little community clustered at their base.

The railroad track lined one side of the main street, while business blocks and public houses were ranged on the opposite side. Here the garb of the Pony Riders failed to attract the same attention that it had done further east. There were many others on the station platform whose clothes and general get-up were similar to those of the boys.

But as they descended from the sleeping car, their arms full of their belongings, each carrying a rifle in a case, they caught sight of a man who instantly claimed their attention. He was fully sixty years old, standing straight as a tree and wearing a soft black felt hat, a white shirt and a wing collar. From his chin, extend almost back to the ears, there stood a growth of white bristling whiskers. As he tilted his head backward in an apparent effort to stand still more erect, the whiskers stood out almost at right angles, giving him a most ferocious appearance.

Tad felt a tug at his sleeve. He turned to find the big eyes of Chunky Brown gazing up into his face.

"Is that the Wild Man of the Canyon?" whispered Stacy.

"I don't know. He looks as if he might be a Senator, or --- "

"Any of you boys know where we can find Jim Nance?" interrupted the Professor.

"I reckon we do," drawled a cowboy.

"Well?" urged the Professor somewhat irritably.

"Wal?" answered the cowboy.

"Will you please tell us where we may find him, pardner?" spoke up Tad, observing how the land lay and wishing to head off friction.

"I reckon that's him," answered the cowboy, pointing to the straight, athletic figure of the old man.

Tad grinned at Chunky.

"That's our guide, Bub."

"He looks fierce enough to be a man eater."

"I'm afraid of him," whispered Stacy. "He's mysterious looking, too; like the Canyon."

Professor Zepplin strode up to the old man.

"Mr.Nance, I believe."

"Y-a-a-s," drawled the old man.

The Professor introduced himself, then one by one called the boys up and presented them, the old man gazing keenly with twinkling, searching eyes into the face of each one presented to him. Chunky said "ouch" when Nance squeezed his hand, then backed off.

"This is Mr.Nance, the gentleman who is to be our guide," announced Professor Zepplin.

"We're all glad to see you, Mr.Nance," chorused the Pony Riders.

"Ain't all tenderfeet, eh?" quizzed the guide.

"No, not exactly. They have been out for some time.

They are pretty well used to roughing it," declared the Professor.

"Good idea. They'll think they haven't before they get through with the old Grand."

"How about our ponies?" asked Tad. "Have you engaged them?"

"You pick 'em out. I'll take yon to corral after you've had your dinner."

All hands walked across the street to a hotel, where they sat down to the first satisfying meal they had eaten since leaving home.

"This beats the spirit meals we've been having on board the train," announced Stacy, his eyes roving longingly over the heaped up dishes.

"Don't lick your chops," cautioned Ned. "There are some polite folks here, as you can see.

"What's that you said about spirit meals?" quizzed the guide after they had gotten started with their dinner.

"The kind a fellow I knew used to make for his men on the farm," answered Stacy promptly.

"Tell us about it. I never heard you mention it," urged Tad.

"He fed his men mostly on spirit soup. Ever hear of spirit soup?"

"I never did. Any of you boys ever hear of spirit soup?"

The Pony Riders shook their heads. They were not particularly interested in Chunky's narration. Ned frowned and went on with his dinner.

"Well, this fellow used to make it. He had barrels of the stuff, and --- "

"How is the chuck made?" demanded Jim Nance.

"I'll tell you. To make spirit soup you catch a snipe. Then you starve him to death. Understand?"

Nance nodded.

"After you've starved him to death you hang him up on the sunny side of the house till he becomes a shadow. A shadow, you understand? Well, after he's become a shadow you let the shadow drop into a barrel of rainwater. The result is spirit soup. Serve a teaspoonful a day as directed," added Stacy, coming to a sudden stop as Ned trod on his toes with a savage heel.

Jim Nance's whiskers stood out, the ends trembling as if from the agitation of their owner, causing Chunky to shrink within himself.

"Very unseemly, young man," rebuked the Professor.

"It seems so," muttered Walter under his breath; then all hands laughed heartily.

The meal being finished, Nance ordered a three-seated buckboard brought around. Into this the whole outfit piled until the bottom of the vehicle bent almost to the ground.

"Will it hold?" questioned the Professor apprehensively.

"I reckon it will if it doesn't break. We'll let the fat boy walk if we've got too big a load," Nance added, with a twinkle.

"No, I'll ride, sir," spoke up Stacy promptly. "I'm very delicate and I'm not allowed to walk, because --- "

"How far is it out to the corral, Mr.Nance?" questioned Tad.

"'Bout a mile as the hawk flies. We'll be there in a jiffy."

It appeared that all arrangements had been made by Mr.Perkins for the stock, through a bank in Flagstaff, where he had deposited funds to cover the purchase of stock and stores for the trip through the Canyon. This the Professor understood. There remained little for the boys to do except for each to pick out the pony be fancied.

They looked over the mustangs in the corral, asking the owner about this and that one.

"I'll take that one," said Chunky, indicating a mild-eyed pinto that stood apparently half asleep.

The owner of the herd of mustangs smiled.

"Kind and sound, isn't he?" questioned the fat boy.

"Oh, he's sound all right."

"Do you know how to handle a pinto, boy?" questioned Nance.

"Do I? Of course I do. Haven't I been riding the toughest critters on the ranges of the Rockies for years and years? Don't I know how to rope anything that ambles on four legs? Well, I guess! Gimme that rope. I'll show you how to fetch a sleepy pinto out of his dreams."

The black that Chunky coveted seemed, at that moment, to have opened his eyes ever so little, then permitted the eyelids to droop. It was not a good sign as Tad viewed it, and the Pony Rider was an excellent horseman.

"Better be careful, Chunky," he warned. "Shan't I rope him for you?"

"I guess not. If I can't rope him I'd like to see you do it."

"Sail in. You know best," answered Tad, with a grin, winking at Ned and the Professor. Jim Nance appeared to take only a passive interest in the matter. He might have his say later provided his advice were needed.

Chunky ran his rope through his hands, then grasping the hondo, strode boldly into the corral.

"I reckon it's time we were climbing the fence," announced Tad.

"I reckon it is," agreed the guide, vaulting to the top

rail, which action was followed by the other two boys, only the owner of the herd and Professor Zepplin remaining inside the corral with Stacy.

Suddenly Stacy let go the loop of his lariat. It dropped over the head of the sleepy pinto. The pinto, at the touch of the rope, sprang into sudden life. Then things began to happen in that corral. Stacy Brown was the center of the happenings.

CHAPTER III

TENDERFEET SHOW THEIR SKILL

"Woof!" exclaimed Ned Rector.

"Oh!" cried Walter Perkins.

"Good boy! Hang on!" shouted Tad encouragingly.

It is doubtful whether Stacy heard either the words of warning or those of encouragement from Tad, for at that moment Stacy's feet were up in the air. The pinto had leaped forward like a shot the instant it felt the touch of the rope. Of course Chunky, who had clung to the rope, went along at the same rate of speed.

A great cloud of dust rose from the corral. The mustang was darting here and there, bucking, squealing and kicking. In a moment most of the other mustangs were doing likewise. The owner of the herd, calling to the Professor, darted out, leaving one bar of the fence down. Professor Zepplin, becoming confused, missed his way and found himself penned into one corner at the far side, almost the center of a circle of kicking mustangs.

Tad saw the danger of their companion almost at once. The lad leaped down, and darting among the kicking animals, made his way toward the Professor just as Stacy's mustang leaped the bars. Stacy's toes caught the top rail, retarding his progress for the briefest part of a second, then he shot out into the air after the racing mustang.

"Leggo!" roared the boys.

"Let go!" shouted the guide. "The little fool! Doesn't he know enough to come in out of the wet?"

"You'll find he doesn't, sir. Your troubles have only just begun. You'll be demanding an increase of wages before you have followed Stacy Brown for a full twenty-four hours," prophesied Ned.

In the meantime Tad had reached the Professor, regardless of the flying hoofs about him. With his rope the boy drove the animals off just in time. Somehow they seemed to have taken it into their heads that the Professor was responsible for their having been disturbed and they were opening their hoof batteries upon him. They gave way before the resolute young Pony Rider almost at once. They recognized that this slender young plainsman and mountaineer was unafraid.

The Professor was weak in the knees by the time he had been led out.

"I didn't know you were in there," apologized Nance.

"Where's Stacy?" was the Professor's first question.

"He's gone by the air line," answered Walter.

While all this had been taking place Chunky had continued in his mad flight for a short distance. He had a long hold on the rope by which the mustang was hauling him. The wary beast, espying a tree whose limbs hung low, changed his course and darted under the lowest of the limbs. Its intention was plain to those who knew the habits of these gentle beasts. The mustang intended to "wipe" the Pony Rider boy free of the line.

Just before reaching the low-hanging limb the pinto darted to one side, then to the other after an almost imperceptible halt. The result was the rope was drawn under the low limb. A quick leap on the part of the mustang, that exhibited almost human intelligence by this manoeuvre, caused Chunky to do a picturesque flop over the limb, falling flat on his back on the other side. This brought the mustang to a quick stop, for the rope had taken a firm hitch around the limb.

The sudden jolt and stoppage of his progress threw the mustang on his nose, where he poised for a few seconds, then he too toppled over on his back.

The owner of the herd was screaming with, merriment, Jim Nance was slapping his sides as he ran, while the Professor was making for the fat boy with long strides.

Tad reached Stacy first. The fat boy lay blinking, looking up at him. Stacy's clothes were pretty well torn, though his body did not seem to be harmed beyond the loss of considerable skin.

"Let me have that rope," commanded Tad.

"N-n-no you don't."

"Let me have that rope, I tell you. I'll attend to the pinto for you."

"Here, give it to me," ordered Jim Nance, reaching for the rope which Tad Butler had taken.

"I can handle him, Mr.Nance."

The "handling" was not easy. Tad was hauled over the best part of an acre of ground ere he succeeded finally in getting an opportunity to cast his own rope. When, however, he did make the cast, the rope caught the pinto by a hind foot, sending the stubborn little beast to the ground. Then Tad was jerked this way and that as the animal sought to kick the foot free.

"Grab the neck rope some of you," he cried.

Nance was the first to obey the command. It was the work of but a moment temporarily to subdue the pinto.

"Take him back. We don't want the critter," ordered the guide.

"I -- I want him," declared Stacy, limping up to the former sleepy beast.

"I'll break him so I guess Stacy can ride him," said Tad. "Ned, will you fetch my saddle and bridle? I can't let go here just yet. Has this fellow ever been ridden?" demanded the boy, looking up at the owner.

"I reckon he has, but not much."

"Why did you let Brown rope the pinto, then?"

"He said he wanted him."

"Let him up," directed Tad. The mustang had another spell, but ere he had finished his bucking Tad had skillfully thrown the saddle on and made fast the saddle girth at the risk of his own life. Next came the bridle, which was not so easily put in place. It was secured at last, after which the lad stepped back to wipe the perspiration from his face and forehead. Dark spots on his khaki blouse showed where the sweat had come through the tough cloth.

"Now I'll ride him," Butler announced.

For the next quarter of an hour there followed an exhibition that won the admiration of all who saw it. All the bucking and kicking that the pinto could do failed to unseat Tad Butler. When finally he rode back to the group, Mr.Mustang's head was held straight out. Once more the sleepy look had come into his eyes, but it was not the same crafty look that had been there before. He was conquered, at least for the time being.

"Now, Chunky, you may try him."

"What do you think of that for riding?" demanded Stacy, turning to the guide.

"Oh, he'll ride one of these days," answered the guide.

"I believe you're a grouch," snorted the fat boy, as he swung into the saddle, quickly thrusting his toes into the stirrups, expecting to be bucked up into the air.

But nothing of the sort followed. The mustang was as meek as could be. Stacy rode the animal up and down the field until satisfied that the pinto was thoroughly broken. Stacy was an object of interest to all. He was a very much banged-up gentleman, nor was Tad so very far behind him in that respect.

Young Butler chose for his mount a mustang with a white face. Already Tad had decided to call him Silver Face. The two very quickly came to an understanding, after a lively but brief rustle about the enclosure. After this Tad roped out the pintos for the others of his party. This done, the boys took their mustangs out into the field, where they tried them out. The spectators were then treated to an exhibition of real riding, though the Pony Riders were not doing this for the sake of showing off. They wanted to try their mounts out thoroughly before deciding to keep those they had chosen.

At last they decided that the stock could stand as picked out, with the exception of Walter Perkins's mustang, which went lame shortly after the boy had started off with him.

"I guess we are all right now," announced Tad, riding up to where the Professor and Jim Nance were standing. "Has either of you any suggestions to offer?"

"Hain't got no suggestions to offer to the likes of you," grumbled the guide. "Where'd you learn to ride like that?"

"Oh, I don't know. It came natural, I guess," replied Tad simply. "The others ride as well as I do."

"Then we'll be moving. I reckon you are figgering on gitting started to-day?"

"Yes, we might as well be on our way as soon as you are ready, Mr. Nance," agreed the Professor.

"How about the pack train?" asked Tad.

"The mules are all ready," answered the guide.

The lads rode their new horses back to Flagstaff. None cared to ride in the buckboard long as there was a horse to ride. Even the Professor thought he would feel at home in the saddle once more. Nance observed that though Professor Zepplin was not the equal of the Pony Riders on horseback, yet he was a good man in the saddle. Nance was observing them all. He knew they would be together for some weeks and it was well to understand the peculiarities of each one of the party at the earliest possible moment.

Reaching town the party found that the entire equipment for the pack train had been gotten in readiness. There remained but to pack the mules and they would be ready for their start. This was done with a will, and about two o'clock in the afternoon the outfit set off over the stage road, headed for the Grand Canyon.

It was a happy party, full of song and jest and joy for that which was before them. The way led through the Coconino Park. Some three miles out they halted at the edge of a dry lake basin, in the centre of which was a great gaping hole. The Professor pointed to it inquiringly.

"There was a lake here up to a few years ago," explained Jim. "Bottom fell out and the water fell in. Ain't no bottom to it now at all"

"Then -- then the water must have leaked out on the other side of the world," stammered Chunky, his eyes big with wonder.

"I reckon it must have soused a heathen Chinee," answered Nance, with a grin.

"Pity it didn't fall out the other way and souse a few guides, eh?" questioned the fat boy, with a good-natured grimace at which Nance laughed inwardly, his shaking whiskers being the only evidence of any emotion whatever.

"Up there is Walnut Canyon," explained Jim. "Cliff dwellers lived up there some time ago."

"Yes, we met some of them down south," nodded Chunky.

"You mean we saw where they once lived long, long ago," corrected Professor Zepplin.

"Yes, we saw where they lived," agreed Stacy.

The way led on through a forest of pines, the trail underfoot being of lava, as hard and smooth as a road could be. They were gradually drawing nearer to Sunset Mountain. After a time they turned off to the right, heading straight for the mountain.

Tad rode back to the Professor to find out where they were going.

"I thought you boys might like to explore the mountain. You will find some things there well worth scientific consideration."

"Yes, sir; that will be fine."

"You know the mountain was once a great volcano."

"How long ago?" interrupted Stacy.

"A few million years or so."

"Mr.Nance must have been a boy in short trousers then," returned Stacy quizzically. The guide's whiskers bristled and stood out straight.

The road by this time had lost its hardness. The ponies' hoofs sank deep into the cinders, making progress slow for the part. They managed to get to the base of the mountain, but the mustangs were pretty well fagged. The animals were turned out for the night after having been hobbled so that they could not stray far away.

"Now each of you will have to carry a pack," announced the guide. "I will tell you what to take."

"Why, where are we going?" asked Tad.

"We are going to spend the night in the crater of the extinct volcano," said the Professor. "Will not that be a strange experience?"

"Hurrah for the crater!" shouted the boys.

"Speaking of volcanoes, I wish you wouldn't open your mouth so wide, Ned. It makes me dizzy. I'm afraid I'll fall in," growled Chunky.

CHAPTER IV

A NIGHT IN THE CRATER

"What, climb that mountain?" demanded Stacy.

"Surely. You are not afraid of a mountain, are you?" demanded Tad.

"I'm not afraid of -- of anything, but I'm delicate, I tell yau."

"Just the same, you'll pack about fifty pounds up the side of that hill," jeered Ned Rector.

The pack mules had not yet come up with their driver. The party foreseeing this, had brought such articles as would be needed for the night. Taking their blankets and their rifles, together with food and wood for a fire, they began the slow, and what proved to be painful, ascent of Sunset Mountain.

A lava field stretched directly in front of them, barring the way. Its forbidding surface had been riven by the elements until it was a perfect chaos of black tumult. By the time the Pony Rider Boys had gotten over this rough stretch, they were ready to sit down and rest. Nance would not permit them to do so. He said they would have barely time to reach the crater before dark, as it was, and that they must make the best speed possible. No one grumbled except Stacy, but it was observed that he plodded along with the others, a few paces to the rear.

The Professor now and then would point to holes in the lava to show where explosions had taken place, bulging the lava around the edge and hurling huge rocks to a considerable distance. As they climbed the mountain proper they found that Sunset, too, had engaged in some gunnery in those far-away ages, as was shown by many lava bombs lying about the base.

The route up the mountain side was over a cider-buried lava flow, the fine cinders under foot soon making progress almost a torture. Tad was the first to stand on his head as his feet went out from under him. Stacy, in a fit of uproarious laughter, did the next stunt, that of literally standing on his right ear. Chunky tried to shout and got his mouth full of cinders.

"I'm going back," howled the fat boy. "I didn't come up here to climb slumbering volcanoes."

"I'll tell you what I'll do, I'll carry you, Stacy," said Tad, smiling and nodding toward the cinder-blackened face of his companion.

"You mean it?"

"Of course I mean it."

"I guess I can walk. I'm not quite so big a baby as that."

"I thought so. Have your fun. If you get into trouble

you know your friend, Tad Butler, is always on the job."

"You bet I do. But this is an awful climb."

It was all of that. One step upward often meant a slide of several short steps backward. The Professor's face was red, and unuttered words were upon his lips. Jim Nance was grinning broadly, his whiskers bobbing up and down as he stumbled up the side of Old Sunset.

"I reckon the tenderfeet will get enough of it before they get to the Canyon," chuckled the guide.

"Say, Mr.Nance, we don't want to Mister you all the time. What shall we call you for short?" asked Tad Butler.

"Anything you want."

"What d'ye say if we call you Whiskers?" called Stacy.

"Stacy!" rebuked the Professor sternly.

"Oh, let the little tenderfoot rant. He's harmless. Call me Whiskers, if it does ye any good."

"I'm no tenderfoot," protested Chunky.

"Nor be I all whiskers," returned the guide, whereat Chunky's face turned red.

"I guess we'll call you Dad, for you'll have to be our dad for some time to come," decided Tad.

"That'll be all right, providing it suits the fat little tenderfoot."

Stacy did not reply to this. He was having too much trouble to keep right side up just then to give heed to anything else.

"Go zig-zag. You'll never get to the top this way," called Tad. "You know how a switchback railroad works? Well, go as nearly like a switch-back as possible."

"That's a good idea," agreed Dad. "You'll get there quicker, as the young gentleman says."

Tad looked at his companions, grinning broadly. As they got nearer to the top the color of the cinders changed from black to a brick red. They began to understand why the peak of Sunset always presented such a rosy appearance. It was due to the tint of the cinders that had been thrown from the mouth of the volcano ages ago.

"We have now entered the region of perpetual sunset," announced the Professor.

Chunky took advantage of the brief halt to sit down. He slid back several feet on the treacherous footing.

Still further up the mountain took on a rich yellow color, but near the rim it was almost white. It was a wonderful effect and caused the Pony Riders to gaze in awe. But darkness was approaching rapidly. The guide ordered them to be on the way, because he desired to reach the rim of the crater while they still were able to see. What his reasons were the boys did not know.

They took for granted that Dad knew his business, which Dad did. He had spent many years in this rough country and knew it well. The Grand Canyon was his home. He lived in it the greater part of the year. When winter came, Dad, with his mustang, his cattle and equipment would descend into the Grand Canyon far from snow and bitter cold into a land of perpetual summer, where, beside the roaring Colorado, he would spend the winter alone with his beloved Canyon.

Dad's was a strange nature. He understood the moods of the great gash in the plateau; he seemed literally to be able to translate the mysterious moans and whispers of the wind as it swirled between the rocky walls and went shrieking up the painted sides of the gulches.

But of all this the boys knew nothing as yet. It was all to be revealed to them later.

"You'll have a look over the country tomorrow," said Dad.

"Where is the Canyon?" asked Tad, eager for a view of the wonderful spot.

"You'll get a glimpse of it in the morning. You'll know the place when you get to it. Here we be at the top. There's the hole."

Chunky peered into the crater rather timidly.

"How do you get down?" he asked.

"Slide," answered Ned.

"I can do that, but what's at the bottom?"

"The same thing. Cinders and lava," answered Tad. "What would you expect to find in a volcano?"

"I'd never expect to find Stacy Brown in one, and I'm not sure that I'm going to."

"All hands follow me. There's no danger," called the guide, shouldering his pack and leaping and sliding down the sharp incline. He was followed by the boys with shouts of glee. They went tumbling head over heels, laughing, whooping, letting off their excess steam. The Professor's grim face relaxed in a smile; Dad's eyes twinkled.

"We'll take it out of them by and by," he confided to the Professor.

"You don't know them," answered Professor Zepplin. "Better men than you or I have tried it. Remember, they are young. We are old men. Of course, it is different with you. You are hardened to the work, still I think they could tire both of us out."

"We'll see about that."

"Whoop-e-e!" came the voice of Tad Butler far below them. "I'm at the bottom. Any wild animals down here, Dad?"

"Only one at present. There'll be three more in a minute."

"Six, you mean," laughed Tad.

The others had soon joined him.

"How far are we from the surface?" asked Walter.

"About five hundred feet down. We're in the bowels of the mountain for sure, kid," answered the guide.

"That's pretty tough on the mountain. I'm afraid it will have a bad case of indigestion," laughed Tad.

"You needn't be. It has swallowed tougher mouthfuls than you are," returned the guide, ever ready with an answer.

"Dad's able to give as good as you send," laughed Ned.

"That's good. All the better for us," nodded Tad. "What about some light?"

"Unload the wood from your packs. This is where you are glad you did pack some stuff."

In a few minutes a fire was blazing, lighting up the interior of the crater. The boys found themselves in a circular opening of almost terrifying roughness and something like a quarter of a mile across. Here, in ages past, the forces of Nature had been at work with fearful earnestness. Weird shadows, mysterious shapes, somewhat resembling moving figures, were thrown by the flickering blaze of the camp fire. While the boys were exploring the crater Dad was busy getting the supper ready, talking with Professor Zepplin as he worked.

The voices of the boys echoed from side to side of the crater, sounding strange and unreal. The call to supper put an end to their explorations. They sat down with keen edges to their appetites. It was their first meal in the open on this journey. All were in high spirits.

"I think we should agree upon our work for the future," declared the Professor.

"Work?" exclaimed Chunky, opening wide his big eyes.

"Yes. It is not going to be all play during this trip."

"We are willing to do our share," answered Ned.

"Yes, of course we are," chorused Walt and Stacy, though there was no enthusiasm in the fat boy's tone.

"I am of the opinion that you boys should take turns in cooking the meals, say one boy to cook for an entire day, another to take the job on the following day."

"I'll cook my own," declared the guide. "No tenderfoot experiments in my chuck."

"They know how to cook, Mr.Nance," explained the Professor.

"All right; they may cook for you," said the guide, with a note of finality in his tone. He glanced up at the sky, held out his hand and shook his head. Tad observed the movement.

"What is it?" asked the boy.

"It's going to snow," said Dad.

Tad laughed, glancing at his companions.

"What, snow in June?" questioned Stacy.

"You must remember that you are a good many thousand feet up," the Professor informed him.

"Up? I thought I was down in a crater."

"You are both up and down," spoke up Tad.

"Yes, I'm usually up and down, first standing on my feet then on my head," retorted Stacy. "How are we going to sleep?"

"Same as usual. Pick out your beds, then roll up in your blankets," directed Dad. "You are used to it, eh?"

"Well," drawled Chunky, "I've slept in a good many different kinds of beds, but this is the first time I ever slept in a lava bed."

True to Dad's prophecy, the snow came within half an hour.

"Better turn in before the beds get too wet," advised Dad.

All hands turned in. Sleep did not come to the boys as readily as usual. They had been sleeping in real beds too long. After a time the snow changed to rain in the warmth of the crater. Chunky got up disgustedly.

"I'm tired of sleeping in the bath tub," he declared. "Think I'll move into the hall bedroom."

Chuckles were heard from beneath other blankets, while Stacy, grumbling and growling, fussed about until he found a place that appeared to be to his liking.

"When you get through changing beds perhaps you will give us a chance to go to sleep," called the guide.

Stacy's voice died away to an indistinct murmur. Soon after that quiet settled over the dark hole in the mountain. The rain came down harder than ever, but by this time the Pony Rider Boys were asleep. They neither heard nor felt the water, though every one was drenched to the skin.

Toward morning Tad woke up with a start. He thought something had startled him. Just then an unearthly yell woke the echoes of the crater. Yell upon yell followed for the next few seconds, each yell seeming to be further away than the preceding one, and finally dying out altogether.

"It's Chunky!" shouted Tad, kicking himself free of his blankets and leaping up. "Some thing's happened to Chunky!"

CHAPTER V

TAD LENDS A HELPING HAND

"What is it? What is it?" cried the other boys, getting free of their blankets and in the confusion rolling and kicking about in the cinders.

"What is it?" shouted the Professor, very much excited.

Ned, dragging his blanket after him, had started to run about, not knowing which way to turn nor what had occurred. In the meantime the guide and Tad had started in the direction from which the yells had seemed to come.

"It was this way," shouted Tad.

Ned headed them off running toward the west edge of the crater. All at once a new note sounded. With an unearthly howl Ned Rector disappeared. They heard his voice growing fainter, too, just as Stacy's had done.

"They've fallen in!" cried Tad.

"Everybody stand still!" commanded Dad.

Recognizing that he was right, the others obeyed, with the exception of Tad Butler, who crept cautiously forward, feeling his way with the toes of his boots, that he too might not share the fate of his two companions.

Dad, from somewhere about his person, produced a bundle of sticks which he lighted. He was prepared for just such an emergency. A flickering light pierced the deep shadows, just enough to show the party that two of their number had disappeared.

"There is the place," cried Tad. "It's a hole in the ground. They've fallen in."

"Chunky's always falling in," laughed Walter half hysterically.

With his rope in hand, Tad sprang forward.

"Light this way, please," called Butler. "Hello, down there!" he cried, peering into the hole in the ground.

"Hello!" came back a faint answer from Ned Rector. "Get us out quick."

"What happened?"

"I don't know. Chunky fell in and I fell on him."

"Is he hurt?"

"I don't know. I guess I knocked the wind out of him."

"How far down are you?" demanded Dad peering in, holding his torch low, exposing a hole about six feet square at the top, widening out as it extended downward.

"I -- I don't know. It felt like a mile when I came down. Hurry. Think I want to stay here all night?"

"If Stacy isn't able to help himself, tie the rope around his waist and we will haul him up," directed Tad.

"Serve him right to leave him here," retorted Ned.

"All right, we will leave you both there, if you feel that way," answered Nance grimly.

"He doesn't mean it," said Tad. "Ned must have his joke, no matter how serious the situation may be." Tad lowered his rope, loop first. "Well, how about it?" he called.

"I've made it fast. Haul away." Chunky was something of a heavy weight. It required the combined efforts of those at the top to haul him out. Dragging Stacy to the surface, Tad dropped beside the fat boy, giving him a shake and peering anxiously into his eyes, shouting, "Stacy! Stacy!"

Chunky opened one eye and winked knowingly at Tad.

"Oh, you rascal! You've made us pull until we are out of breath. Why'd you make a dead weight of yourself?"

"Is -- is he all right?" inquired Professor Zepplin anxiously.

"He hasn't been hurt --- "

"Yes, I have. I'm all bunged up -- I'm all shot to pieces. The – the mountain blew up and --- "

"Well, are you fellows going to leave me down here all the rest of the night?" demanded the far-away voice of Ned Rector.

"Yes, you stay there. You're out of the wet," answered Stacy.

"That's a fine way to talk after I have saved your life almost at the expense of my own."

"Pshaw! Saved my life! You nearly knocked it all out of me when you fell on top of me."

"Here comes the rope, Ned," called Tad. "If you can help us a little you will make the haul easier for us."

"I'll use my feet."

"Better take a hitch around your waist in case you should slip," advised Butler.

Ned did so, and by bracing his feet against the side of the rock he was able to aid them not a little in their efforts to haul him to the surface. Ned fixed Stacy with stern eye.

"Were you bluffing all the time?" he demanded.

"Was I bluffing? Think a fellow would need to bluff when a big chump like you fell in on him? I thought the mountain had caved in on me, but it was something softer than a mountain, I guess," added Stacy maliciously.

"What did happen?" demanded Ned, gazing at the hole wonderingly.

"It's one of those thin crusts," announced the guide, examining the broken place in the lava with critical eyes, in which occupation the Professor joined.

"Yes, it was pretty crusty," muttered Chunky.

"You see, sir, this occurs occasionally," nodded the guide, looking up at the grizzled face of Professor Zepplin. "One never knows in this country when the crust is going to give way and let him down. I guess the rain must have weakened the ground."

"And I fell in again," growled Stacy.

"You were bound to fall in sooner or later," answered Tad. "Perhaps it is just as well that you fell in a soft place."

"A soft place?" shouted Stacy. "If you think so, just take a drop in there yourself."

"I thought it was the softest thing I ever fell on," grinned Rector, whereupon the laugh was on Stacy.

There was no more sleep in the camp in the crater of Sunset Peak that night. Nor was there fire to warm the campers. They walked about until daylight. That morning they made a breakfast on cold biscuit and snowballs at the rim of the crater. But as the sun came out they felt well repaid for all that they had passed through on the previous night. Such a vista of wonderful peaks as lay before them none of the Pony Riders ever had gazed upon.

To the west lay the San Francisco Peaks, those ever-present landmarks of northern Arizona. To the south the boys looked off over a vast area of forest and hills, while to the east in the foreground were grouped many superb cinder cones, similar to the one on which they were standing, though not nearly so high. Lava beds, rugged and barren, reached out like fingers to the edge of the plateau as if reaching for the far-away painted desert.

"Where is the Canyon?" asked Tad in a low voice.

"Yonder," said Dad, pointing to the north over an unbroken stretch of forest. There in the dim distance lay the walls of the Grand Canyon, the stupendous expanse of the ramparts of the Canyon stretching as far as the eye could see.

"How far away are they?" asked Tad.

"More than forty miles," answered Dad. "You wait till we get to the edge. You can't tell anything about those buttes now."

"What is a butte -- how did they happen to be called that?" asked Walter.

"A butte is a butte," answered the guide.

"A butte is a bump on the landscape," interjected Stacy.

"A butte is a mound of earth or stone worn away by erosion," answered the Professor, with an assurance that forbade any one to question the correctness of his statement.

"Yes, sir," murmured the Pony Rider Boys. "A wart on

the hand of fair Nature, as it were," added Chunky under his breath.

"Come, we must be on our way," urged Dad. "We want to make half the distance to the Canyon before night. I reckon the pack train will have gone on. We'll have to live on what we have in our saddle bags till we catch up with the train, which I reckon we'll do hard onto noon."

No great effort was required to descend Sunset Mountain. It was one long slide and roll. The boys screamed with delight as they saw the dignified Professor coasting and taking headers down the cinder-covered mountain.

By this time the clothes of the explorers had become well dried out in the hot sun. When they reached the camp they found that the pack train had long since broken camp and gone on.

"Where are the ponies?" cried Walter, looking about.

"I'll get them," answered Dad, circling the camp a few times to pick up the trail.

It will be remembered that the animals had been hobbled on the previous afternoon and turned loose to graze. Dad found the trail and was off on it running with head bent, reminding the boys of the actions of a hound. While he was away Tad cooked breakfast, made coffee and the others showed their appreciation of his efforts by eating all that was placed before them and calling loudly for more. Dad returned about an hour later, riding Silver Face, driving the other mustangs before him. When the boys saw the stock coming in they shouted with merriment. The mustangs had been hobbled by tying their fore feet together. This made it necessary for the animals to hop like kangaroos. The boys named them the kangaroos right then and there.

Tad had some hot coffee ready for Nance by the time Dad got back. The guide forgot that he had declared against eating or drinking anything cooked by the Pony Rider Boys. He did full justice to Tad's cooking, while the rest of the boys stood around watching the guide eat, offering suggestions and remarks. Dad took it all good-naturedly. He would have plenty of opportunities to get back at them. Dad was something of a joker himself, though this fact was suspected only by Tad Butler, who had noted the constantly recurring twinkle in the eyes of the guide.

"We shall hear from Dad one of these days," was Butler's mental conclusion. "All right, we deserve all we get and more, I guess."

Shortly afterwards the party was in the saddle, setting out for their forty-mile ride in high spirits. They hoped to reach their destination early on the following morning. Some of the way was dusty and hot, though the greater part of it was shaded by the giant pines.

They caught up with the pack train shortly before noon, as Nance had said they would. A halt was made and a real meal cooked while the mustangs were watered and permitted to graze at the ends of their ropes. The meal being finished, saddle bags were stocked as the party would not see the pack train again until some time on the following day. Then the journey was resumed again.

The Pony Rider Boys were full of anticipation for what they would see when they reached the Canyon. Dad was in a hurry, too. He could hardly wait until he came in sight of his beloved Canyon. But even with all their expectations the lads had no idea of the wonderful sight in store for them when they should first set eyes on this greatest of Nature's wonders.

That night they took supper under the tall trees, and after a sleep of some three hours, were roughly awakened by the guide, who soon had them started on their way again.

CHAPTER VI

A SIGHT THAT THRILLED

"We'll make camp here for a time, I reckon," announced Dad about two o'clock in the morning.

"I thought we were going on to the Canyon," said Tad.

"We shall see it in the morning," answered the guide somewhat evasively. "You boys turn in now, and get some sleep, for you will want to have your eyes wide open in the morning. But let me give you a tip: Don't you go roaming around in the dark here."

"Why -- why not?" demanded Stacy Brown.

"Oh, nothing much, only we're likely to lose your valuable company if you try it. You have a habit of falling in, I am told. You'll fall in for keeps if you go moseying about in this vicinity."

"Where are we?" asked Butler.

"'Bout half a mile from the El Tovar," answered Nance. "Now you fellows turn in. Stake down the pintos. Isn't safe to let them roam around on two legs."

Tad understood. He knew from the words of Nance

that they were somewhere in the vicinity of the great gash in the earth that they had come so far to see. But he was content to wait until the morrow for the great sight that was before them.

The sun was an hour high before they felt the heavy hand of Jim Nance on their shoulders shaking them awake. The odor of steaming coffee and frying bacon was in the air.

"What -- sunrise?" cried Tad, sitting up and rubbing his eyes.

"And breakfast?" added Ned.

"Real food?" piped Stacy Brown.

"Where do we wash?" questioned Walter.

"You will have to take a sun bath," answered the guide with a twinkle. "There isn't any water near this place. We will find water for the stock later in the morning."

"But where is the Canyon?" wondered Tad.

"You're at it."

"I don't see anything that looks like a canyon," scoffed Ned.

"No, this is a level plateau," returned Tad. "However, I guess Dad knows what he is talking about. I for one am more interested in what I smell just now than anything else."

Chunky sniffed the air.

"Well, it will take more than a smell to satisfy me this morning," declared Chunky, wrinkling his nose.

"This is my day to cook," called Tad. "Why didn't you let me get the breakfast, Mr.Nance?"

"I'm doing the cooking this morning. I've had a long walk and feel fine, so I decided to be the cook, the wrangler and the whole outfit this morning. How do you feel, boys?"

"Fine!" chorused the Pony Riders. "But we thought we should see the Canyon when we woke up this morning."

A quizzical smile twitched the corners of Dad's mouth. Tad saw that the guide had something of a surprise for them. The lad asked no further questions.

Breakfast finished, the boys cleared away the dishes, packing everything as if for a continuation of their journey, which they fully expected to make.

A slight rise of ground lay a few rods ahead of them. Tad started to stroll that way. He halted as a party of men and women were seen approaching from the direction of El Tovar, where the hotel was located.

"Now, gentlemen, you may walk along," nodded the guide, smiling broadly.

"Which way?" asked the Professor.

"Follow the crowd you see there."

They saw the party step up to the rise, then a woman's

scream smote their ears. Tad, thinking something had occurred, dashed forward.

He reached the level plateau on the rise, where his companions saw him halt suddenly, throwing both arms above his head.

The boys started on a run, followed by the professor, who by this time was a little excited.

Then all at once the glorious panorama burst upon them. There at their very feet lay the Grand Canyon. Below them lay the wonder of the world, and more than five thousand feet down, like a slender silver thread, rippled the Colorado.

The first sight of the Canyon affects different persons differently. It overwhelmed the Pony Rider Boys, leaving them speechless. They shrank back as they gazed into the awful chasm at their feet and into which they might have plunged had the hour been earlier, for it had burst upon them almost with the suddenness of the crack of a rifle.

They had thought to see mountains. There were none. What they saw was really a break in the level plateau. From where they stood they looked almost straight down into the abyss for something more than a mile. Gazing straight ahead they saw to the other side of the chasm twelve miles away. To the right and to the left their gaze reached more than twenty miles in each direction.

This great space was filled with gigantic architectural constructions, with amphitheaters, gorges, precipices, walls of masonry, fortresses, terraced up to the level of the eyes, temples, mountain high, all brilliant with horizontal lines of color -- streaks of hues from a few feet to a thousand feet in width, mottled here and there with all the colors of the rainbow.

Such coloring, such harmony of tints the Pony Rider Boys never had gazed on before. It seemed to them as if they themselves were standing in midair looking down upon a new and wonderful world. There was neither laughter nor jest upon the lips of these brown-faced, hardy boys now.

Professor Zepplin slowly took off his hat in homage to what was there at his feet. He wiped the perspiration from his forehead. A glance at Tad Butler showed tear drops glistening on his cheeks. He was trembling. Never before had a more profound emotion taken hold of him. Ned Rector and Walter Perkins's faces wore expressions of fear. No other moment in the lives of the four boys had been like this.

Dad's face shone as with a reflected light from the Canyon that he loved so well, and that had been his almost constant companion for more than thirty years; whose moods he knew almost as well as his own, and whose every smile or frown had its meaning for him.

The travelers each forgot that there was any other human being than himself present. They were drawn sharply to the fact that there were others present, when one of the little party of sight-seers that had come over from the hotel picked up a rock, the weight of which was almost too much for him.

The lads watched him with fascinated eyes. The man swung the rock back and forth a few times, then hurled it over the edge. The Pony Rider Boys waited, actually holding their breath, to catch the report when the rock should strike the bottom.

No report came. It requires some little time for a rock to fall a mile, and when it does land it is doubtful if those at the other end of the mile would hear the report.

The faces of the Pony Riders actually paled. This was indeed the next thing to a bottomless pit. Walter Perkins recalled afterwards that his head had spun dizzily, Ned that he was too frightened to move a muscle.

Suddenly the silence was broken by a shout that was really an agonized yell. The voice was Stacy Brown's.

"Hold me! Somebody hold me!" he screamed

The others glanced at him with disapproving eyes. Could nothing impress Chunky? The fat boy had begun to move forward toward the edge, both hands extended in front of him as to ward off something.

"Hold me! I'm going to jump! Oh, won't somebody hold me?"

Even then only one in that little party appeared to understand. They were paralyzed with amazement and unable to move a muscle. The one who did see and understand was Tad Butler. Chunky was giving way to an irresistible impulse. He was at that instant being drawn toward the terrible abyss.

CHAPTER VII

ON THE RIM OF ETERNITY

Tad caught his breath sharply. He, too, for the instant seemed unable to move. Then all at once he sprang forward, throwing himself upon the fat boy, both going to earth together, locked in a tight embrace.

"Leggo! Leggo!" shrieked Stacy.

The fat boy fought desperately. He had appealed for help; now he refused to accept it. He was possessed with a maddened desire to throw himself into the mile-deep chasm. It was all Tad Butler could do at the moment to keep from being rolled to the rim himself.

Dad, suddenly discovering the situation, ran at full speed toward the struggling boys.

"Grab his legs. I will look out for his shoulders," gasped Tad, sitting down on Chunky's face for a brief respite.

"I'll handle him," said the guide quietly. "They get taken that way sometimes when they first look into the hole."

By this time the others, having shaken off the spell,

started to move toward the scene of the brief conflict. Dad waved them back; then, with Tad holding up the fat boy's shoulders, Dad with Chunky's feet in hand, the two carried him back some distance, where they laid him on the ground. Stacy did not move. His face was ghastly.

"I think he has fainted -- fainted away," stammered Tad.

"Let him alone. He'll be all right in a few minutes," directed the guide.

"What made him do that?" wondered Tad, turning large eyes on Nance.

"He jest couldn't help it. I told you you'd see something, but I didn't think Fatty would be taken quite so hard. You go back."

"No, I'll wait. You perhaps had better look after the others, Ned or the Professor might be taken the same way," answered Tad, with a faint smile.

Nance hurried back. After a time Chunky opened his eyes. He sat up, looking dazed then he reached a feeble hand toward Tad.

"I'd 'a' gone sure, Tad," he said weakly.

"Nonsense!"

"I would, sure."

"Come back and look at it."

"Not for a million, I wouldn't."

"Oh, pooh! Don't be a baby. Come back, I tell you. You've got to get over that fright. We shall have to be around this canyon for some time. If you haven't any nerve, why --- "

"Nerve? Nerve?" queried Stacy, rousing himself suddenly. "Talk about nerve! Don't you think it takes nerve for a fellow to start in to jump off a rock a mile high? Well, I guess it does. Don't you talk to me about nerve."

"There come the others."

The Professor, the guide and the other boys walked slowly up to them at this juncture. Chunky expected that Ned would make fun of him. Ned did nothing of the sort. Both Ned and Walter were solemn and their faces were drawn. They sighed as if they had just awakened from a deep sleep.

"What do you think of it, Professor?" asked Tad, looking up.

"Words fail me."

"I must have another look," announced Butler.

He walked straight to the edge of the rim, then lying flat on his stomach, head out over the chasm, he gazed down into the terrible abyss.

Jim Nance nodded approvingly.

"He's going to love it just the same as I do." The old

man's heart warmed toward Tad Butler in that moment, when Tad, all alone, sought a closer acquaintance with the mystery of the great gash. After a time the others walked back, Dad taking Chunky by the nape of the neck. Perhaps it was the method of approach, or else Chunky, having had his fright, had been cured. At least this time he felt no fear. He was lost in wonder.

"Buck up now!" urged the guide.

"I am bucked. Leggo my neck. I won't make a fool of myself this time, I promise you."

"You can't blame him," said Tad, rising from his perilous position and walking calmly back to them. "I nearly got them myself."

"Got what?" demanded Stacy.

"The jiggers."

"That's it. That describes it."

Professor Zepplin, who had informed himself before starting out, now turned suddenly upon them.

"He's going to give us a lecture. Listen," whispered Tad.

"Young gentlemen, you have, perhaps, little idea of the vastness of that upon which you are now gazing."

"We know it is the biggest thing in the world, Professor," said Ned.

"Imagine, if you can," continued the Professor, without

heeding the interruption, "that this amphitheatre is a real theatre. Allowing twice as much room as is given for the seat of each person in the most comfortable theatre in the world, and you could seat here an audience of two hundred and fifty millions of people. These would all be in the boxes on this side."

The boys opened their eyes at the magnitude of the figures.

"An orchestra of one hundred million pieces and a chorus of a hundred and fifty million voices could be placed comfortably on the opposite side. Can you conceive of such a scene? What do you think of it?"

"I -- I think," stammered Chunky, "that I'd like to be in the box office of that show -- holding on to the ticket money."

Without appearing to have heard Stacy Brown's flippant reply, Professor Zepplin began again.

"Now that you are about to explore this fairy land it is well that you be informed in advance as to what it is. The river which you see down there is the Colorado. As perhaps some of you, who have studied your geography seriously, may know, the river is formed in southern Utah by the confluence of the Green and Grand, intersecting the north-western corner of Arizona it becomes the eastern boundary of Nevada and California, flowing southward until it reaches the Gulf of California."

"Yes, sir," said the boys politely, filling in a brief pause.

"That river drains a territory of some three hundred thousand square miles, and from its source is two thousand miles long. This gorge is slightly more than two hundred miles long. Am I correct in my figures, Mr.Nance?" demanded the Professor, turning to Dad, a "contradict-me-at-your-peril" expression on his face.

"I reckon you are, sir."

"The river has a winding way --- "

"That's the way with rivers," muttered Chunky to himself.

"Millions of years have been consumed in the building of this great Canyon. In that time ten thousand feet of non-conformable strata have been deposited, elevated, tilted, and washed away; the depression of the Canyon Surface serving for the depositing of Devonian, Lower Carboniferous, Upper Carboniferous, Permian, Triassic, Jurassic, Cretaceous; the formation of the vast eocene lake and its total disappearance; the opening of the earth's crust and the venting from its angry stomach the foul lavas -- the mind reels and whirls and grows dizzy --- "

"So do I," almost shouted Chunky, toppling over in a heap. "Quit it! You make me sea sick --- "

"I am amazed," bristled the Professor. "I am positively amazed that a young gentleman -- "

"It was the whirling, reeling suggestion that made his head swim, I think, Professor," explained Tad, by way of helping out the fat boy.

The lecture was not continued from that point just then. The Professor postponed the rest of his recital until a more opportune time.

"Will you go down to-day, or will you wait?" asked the guide.

"I think we shall find quite enough here on the edge of the rim to occupy our minds for the rest of the day, Nance," returned the Professor.

The boys agreed to this. They did not feel as if they ever would want to leave the view that fascinated and held them so enthralled. That day they journeyed over to the hotel for dinner. The guests at the quaint hotel were much interested in the Pony Rider Boys, and late in the afternoon quite a crowd came over to visit Camp Grand, as the lads had named their camp after the pack train had arrived and the tents were pitched.

There were four tents all pitched in a row facing the Canyon, the tents in a straight line. In front the American flag was planted, the camp fire burning about midway of the line and in front, so that at night it would light up the entire company street.

They cooked their own supper, Tad attending to this. But the boys were too full of the wonderful things they had seen that day to feel their usual keen-edged appetite.

The dishes put away, the Professor having become deeply absorbed in an argument with some gentlemen from the hotel regarding the "processes of deposition and subsidence of the uplift," Tad slipped away, leaving his chums listening to the conversation. Dad was also listening in open-mouthed wonder that any human being could use such long words as were being passed back and forth without choking to death. He was, however, so absorbed in the conversation that he did not at the moment note Butler's departure. Tad passed out of sight in the direction of the Canyon.

After a few moments had passed, Dad stirred the fire, then he too strolled off toward the rim. Tad, fearless, regardless of the peril to himself, was lying flat on his stomach gazing down over the rim, listening to the mysterious voices of the Canyon.

"I don't want you to be here, boy," said the guide gently.

Though he had approached silently, without revealing his presence, Tad never moved nor started, the tone was so gentle, and then again the boy's mind was full of other things.

"Why don't you want me here, Mr.Nance?" Dad squatted down on the very edge of the rim, both feet banging over, one arm thrown lightly over Tad's shoulders.

"You might fall."

"What about yourself? You might fall, too. You are in more danger than am I."

"Dad is not afraid. The Canyon is his home -- "

"You mean you live here?"

"The greater part of the year."

"Where?"

"Some day I will show you. It is far, far down in my beloved Canyon, where the foot of the white man seldom strays. Have you heard the strange voices of Dad's friend?"

"Yes, Dad, I have heard. I hear them now."

Both fell silent. The far away roar of the turbulent waters of the Colorado was borne to their listening ears. There were other sounds, too, mysterious sounds that came like distant moans, rising and falling, with here and there one that sounded like a sob.

"The spirit of the Canyon is sad to-night," murmured Dad.

"Why, Dad, that was the wind sighing through the Canyon."

"Yes, I know, but back of it all there is life, there is the very spirit of life. I don't know how to explain it, but I feel it deep down inside of me. I think you do, too."

"Yes, Dad, I do."

"I know you do. It's a living thing to me, kid, as it will be to you after you know their voices better and they come to know you. All those people," with a sweeping gesture toward the hotel where music and song were heard, "miss it all. What they see is a great spectacle. To see the Grand Canyon is to feel it in your heart. Seeing it in any other way is not seeing it at all."

"And do you live down there alone?"

"Yes. Why not?"

"I should think you would long for human companionship."

"What, with my beloved Canyon to keep me company? No, I am never lonely," added Jim Nance simply. "I shall live and die there -- I hope, and I'll be buried down there somewhere There are riches down there too. Gold -- much gold --- "

"Why don't you go after it --- "

Dad shook his head.

"It would be like robbing a friend. No, you may take the gold if you can find it, but Dad, never. See, the moon is up. Look!"

It was a new scene that Tad gazed upon. Vishnu Temple, the most wonderful piece of architecture in the Canyon, had turned to molten silver. This with Newberry Terrace, Solomon's Throne, Shinto Temple and other lesser ones stood out like some wonderful Oriental city.

All at once the quiet of the beautiful scene was disturbed by a bowl that was plainly the voice of Stacy Brown. Stacy, his big eyes missing little that had been going on about him, had after a time stolen away after Tad and the guide. His curiosity had been aroused by their departure and still more by the time they had been gone. Chunky determined to go out and investigate for himself.

He had picked his way cautiously toward the Canyon

when he halted suddenly, his eyes growing large at what he saw.

"Yeow! Look!" cried the fat boy.

Both Jim Nance and Tad sprang up. Those in the camp heard the shout and ran toward the rim, fearing that some harm had befallen Stacy.

CHAPTER VIII

THE CITY IN THE SKIES

"What has happened now?" cried Tad, running forward.

"Look, look!"

Tad and the guide turned at the same instant gazing off across the Canyon. At first Tad saw nothing more than he had already seen.

"I -- I don't --- "

"It's up there in the skies. Don't you see?" almost shouted Stacy, pointing.

"What is it? What is it?" shouted the others from the camp, coming up on a run.

Then Tad saw. High up in the skies, as plainly outlined as if it were not more than a mile away, was reflected a city. Evidently it was an Eastern city, for there were towers, domes and minarets, the most wonderful sight he had ever gazed upon.

"A -- a mirage!"

"Yes," said Dad. "We see them here some times, but not often. My friends down there are showing you many things this night. Yes they never do that unless they are pleased. The spirit of the Canyon is well pleased. I was sure it would be."

By this time the others had arrived. All were uttering exclamations of amazement, only Tad and Dad being silent and thoughtful. For several minutes the reflection hung suspended in the sky, then a filmy mist was drawn before it like a curtain.

"Show's over," announced Chunky. "That billion orchestra will now play the overture backwards."

"Most remarkable thing I've ever seen," announced the Professor, whereupon he entered into a long scientific discussion on mirages with the gentlemen from the hotel.

Tad and the guide followed them slowly back to camp. The conversation soon became general. Dad was drawn into it, but he spoke no more about the things he and Butler had talked of out on the rim of the Canyon, literally hanging between heaven and earth.

"Well, what about to-morrow, Mr.Nance?" questioned the Professor, after the visitors had left them.

"I reckoned we'd go down Bright Angel Trail," answered the guide.

"Do we take the pack train with us?"

Nance shook his head.

"Too hard a trail. Besides we can't get anywhere with the mules on that trail. We've got to come back up here."

"Aren't we going into the Canyon to stay?" asked Walter.

"Yes. We'll either go down Bass Trail or Grand View. We can get the pack mules down those trails, but on the Bright Angel we'll have to leave the pintos before we get to the bottom and climb down."

"Any Indians down there?" asked Ned.

"Sure, there are Indians."

"What's that, Indians?" demanded Stacy, alive with quick interest.

"Yes. There's a Havasupai camp down in Cataract Canyon, then there are always some Navajos gunning about to make trouble for themselves and everybody else. The Apaches used to come down here, too, but we don't see them very often except when the Havasus give a peace dance or there's something out of the ordinary going on."

"And do -- do we see them?"

"See the Indians? Of course you'll see them."

"Are they bad?" asked the fat boy innocently.

"All Indians are bad. However, the Havasus won't bother you if you treat them right. Don't play any of your funny, sudden tricks on them or they might resent it. They're a peaceable lot when they're let alone."

"One of the gentlemen who were here this evening told me the Navajos, quite a party of them, had made a camp down near Bright Angel Gulch, if you know where that is," spoke up Professor Zepplin.

Dad pricked up his ears at this.

"Then they aren't here for any good. The agent will be after them if they don't watch out. I'll have a look at those bucks and see what rascality they're up to now," said Nance.

"Any chance of a row?" questioned Ned.

"No, no row. Leastwise not for us. Your Uncle Sam will look after those gentlemen if they get gay. But they won't. It will be some crooked little trick under cover -- taking the deer or something of the sort."

"Will we get any chance to shoot deer?" asked Walter.

"You will not unless you are willing to be arrested. It's a closed season from now till winter. I saw a herd of antelope off near Red Butte this afternoon."

"You must have eyes like a hawk," declared Stacy, with emphasis.

"Eyes were made to see with," answered Nance shortly.

"And ears to hear, and feet to foot with, and --- "

"Young men, it is time you were in bed. I presume

Mr.Nance will be wanting to make an early start in the morning," said the Professor.

"If we are to get back the same day we'll have to start about daybreak. It's a hard trail to pack. You'll be ready to stretch your legs when we get back to-morrow night."

The boys were not ready to use those same legs when they were turned out at daybreak. There was some grumbling, but not much as they got up and made ready their hurried breakfast. In the meantime Nance had gotten together such provisions as he thought they would need. These he had packed in the saddle bags so as to distribute the weight.Shortly after breakfast they made a start, Dad going first, Tad following close behind.

The first two miles of the Bright Angel Trail was a sort of Jacob's ladder, zigzagging at an unrelenting pitch. Most of the way the boys had to dig their knees into the sides of their mounts to prevent slipping over the animals' necks.

"This is mountain climbing backwards," jeered Stacy.

"I don't know, but I guess I like it the other way," decided Walter, looking down a dizzy slope.

"I hope my pony doesn't stumble," answered Ned.

"You won't know much about it if he does," called Tad over his shoulder.

"Never mind. We'll borrow an Indian basket to bring you home," laughed Stacy in a comforting voice.

The trail was the roughest and the most perilous they had ever essayed. The ponies were obliged to pick their way over rocks, around sharp, narrow corners, where the slightest misstep would send horse and rider crashing to the rocks hundreds of feet below. But to the credit of the Pony Rider Boys it may be said that not one of them lost his head for an instant.

"How did this trail ever get such a name?" asked Tad of the guide.

"Yes, I don't see any signs of angels hereabouts," agreed Chunky.

"You never will unless you mend your ways," flung back Nance.

"Oh, I don't know. There are others."

"On the government maps this is called Cameron Trail, but it is best known by its original name, Bright Angel, named after Bright Angel creek which flows down the Canyon."

"Where is Bright Angel Canyon?" asked Tad.

"That's where the wild red men are hanging out," said Stacy.

"That's some distance from here. We shan't see it until some days later," replied the guide. "This, in days long ago, was a Havasupai Indian trail. You see those things that look like ditches?"

"Yes."

"Those were their irrigating canals. They knew how to irrigate a long time before we understood its advantages. Their canals conveyed large volumes of water from springs to the Indian Gardens beyond here. Yonder is what is known as the Battleship Iowa," said the guide, pointing to the left to a majestic pile of red sandstone that capped the red wall of the Canyon.

"Don't shoot," cried Stacy, ducking.

"You'll be shooting down into the Colorado," warned Nance. "You'd better watch out."

The rock indicated did very much resemble a battleship. The boys marveled at it. Then a little further on they came upon a sandstone plateau from which they could look down into the Indian Garden, another plateau rich with foliage, green grass and a riot of flowers. It was like looking into a bit of the tropics.

"Here is the worst piece of trail we have yet found," called Nance. "Go carefully," he directed when they reached the "blue lime." For the next few minutes, until they had passed over this most dangerous portion, little was said. The riders were too busy watching out for their own safety, the Professor, examining the different strata of rocks that so appeal to the geologist. He was entranced with what he beheld about him. Professor Zepplin had no time in which to enjoy being nervous.

From there on to the Garden they rode more at ease in the "Boulder Bed," where lay large blocks of rock of many shapes and sizes that had rolled from some upper strata. Small shrubs and plants grew on every hand, many-hued lizards and inquisitive swifts darted across the trail, acting as if they resented the intrusion.

Chunky regarded the lizards with disapproving eyes. But his thoughts were interrupted by the voice of the guide pointing out the Temple of Isis that looks down six thousand feet into the dark depths of the inner abyss, surrounded by innumerable smaller buttes. The wonderful colorings of the rocks did not suffer by closer inspection; in fact, the colors appeared to be even brighter than when viewed from the rim a few thousand feet above them.

Indian Garden was a delight. They wanted to tarry there, but were allowed to do so only long enough to permit horses and riders to refresh themselves with the cold water that trickled down through the canals from the springs far above.

Reaching the end of Angel Plateau they gazed down a sheer descent of twelve hundred feet into the black depths of the inner gorge, where flowed the Colorado with a sullen roar that now was borne plainly to their ears.

"It sounds as I have heard the rapids at Niagara do," declared Chunky somewhat ambiguously.

"All off!" called the guide.

"What's off?" demanded Chunky.

"Dismount."

"Is this as far as we go?" questioned Tad.

"It is as far as we go on the pintos. We have to climb

down the rest of the way, and it's a climb for your life."

The boys gazed down the wall to the river gorge. The prospect did not look very inviting.

"I guess maybe I'd better stay here and mind the 'tangs'," suggested Stacy, a remark that brought smiles to the faces of the other boys.

"No, you'd be falling off if we left you here," declared Dad. "You'll go along with us."

Before starting on the final thousand feet of the descent the trappings were removed from the horses, after which the animals were staked down so that they might not in a moment of forgetfulness fall over the wall and be dashed to pieces on the rocks below.

Dad got out his climbing ropes, the boys watching the preparations with keen interest.

"Are you going down, Professor?" asked Tad smilingly.

"Certainly I am going down. I for one have no intention of remaining to watch the stock," with a grim glance in Chunky's direction. Chunky saw fit to ignore the fling at him. He was gazing off across the chasm at the Temple of Isis, which at that moment absorbed his full attention.

"Now I guess we are ready," announced the guide finally. "I will go first. In places it will be necessary to cling to the rope. Don't let go. Then, in case you stumble, you won't get the nasty fall that you otherwise would be likely to get."

Away up, just below the Indian Garden, they picked up the slender trail that led on down to the roaring river. They had never had quite such a climb, either up or down.

Every time they looked down they saw a possible fall upon rough, blade-like granite edges.

"We'd be sausage meat if we landed on those," declared Chunky.

"You are likely to go through the machine if you don't pay closer attention to your business," answered Dad.

Carefully, cautiously, laboriously they lowered themselves one by one over the steep and slippery rocks, down, down for hundreds of feet until they stood on the ragged edge of nowhere, a direct drop of several hundred feet more before them.

The guide knew a trail further on, so they crept along the smooth wall of the Canyon with scarcely room to plant their feet. A misstep meant death.

"Three hundred feet and we shall be there," came the encouraging voice of the guide. "Half an hour more."

"I could make it half a minute if I wanted to," said Stacy. "But I don't want to. I feel it my duty to stay and look after my friends."

"Yes, your friends need you," answered Ned sarcastically. "If they hadn't I never should have pulled you out of the hole in the crater."

"I was just wondering how Chunky could resist the temptation of falling in here. He'll never have a better opportunity for making a clean job of said Walter.

"He has explained why," replied Tad. "We need him. Of course we do. We need him every hour --- "

"And a half," added Ned.

The roar of the river became louder as they descended. Now they were obliged to raise their voices to make themselves heard. The Professor was toiling and sweating, but making no complaint of the hardships. He was plucky, as game as any of those hardy boys for whom he was the companion, and they knew it.

"Hold on here!" cried Stacy, halting.

All turned to see what was wrong.

"I want to know -- I want to know before I take another step."

"Well, what do you want to know?" demanded Tad.

"If it's all this trouble to climb down, I want to know how in the name of Bright Angel Trail we're ever going to be able to climb up again!"

"Fall up, of course," flung back the guide. "You said this was mountain climbing backwards. It'll be that way going back," chuckled the guide.

"And I so delicate!" muttered the lad, gazing up the hundreds of feet of almost sheer precipice. But ere the

Pony Rider Boys scaled those rocks again they would pass through some experiences that were far from pleasurable ones.

CHAPTER IX

CHUNKY WANTS TO GO HOME

Instead of a half hour, as had been prophesied, a full hour elapsed before they reached the bottom of the trail that was practically no trail at all. Tad was sure that the guide couldn't find his way back over the same ground, or rather rock, to save his life, for the boy could find nothing that looked as if the foot of man had ever trodden upon it before. He doubted if any one had been over that particular trail from the Garden on.

As a matter of fact, Dad had led them into new fields. But at last they stood upon the surer foundation of the bottom of the chasm.

"Anyone needs to be a mountain goat to take that journey," said Tad, with a laugh.

"No, a bird would be better," piped Stacy.

"I'd rather be a bug, then I wouldn't have to climb," spoke up Walter.

"Hurrah! Walt's said something," shouted Ned.

By this time Nance and the Professor had walked

along, climbing over boulders, great blocks of stone that had tumbled from the walls above, making their way to the edge of the river.

The others followed, talking together at the tops of their voices, laughing and joking. They felt relieved that the terrible climb had come to an end. As they approached the river, their voices died away. It was a sublime but terrifying spectacle that the Pony Rider Boys gazed upon.

"This is more wonderful than Niagara," finally announced the Professor. "The rapids of the Niagara River would be lost in this turbid stream."

Great knife-like rocks projected from the flood. When the water struck these sharp edges it was cleanly cut, spurting up into the air like geysers, sending a rainbow spray for many yards on either side.

What puzzled the lads more than all else were the great leaping waves that rose without apparent cause from spaces of comparatively calm water. These upturning waves, the guide explained, were the terror of explorers who sought to get through the Canyon in boats.

"Has any one ever accomplished it?" asked Tad.

"Yes; that intrepid explorer, Major J.W.Powell, made the trip in the year 1869, one of the most thrilling voyages that man ever took. Several of his men were lost; two who managed to escape below here were killed by the Indians."

"I think I should like to try it," said Tad thoughtfully.

"You won't, if I have anything to say about the matter," replied Dad shortly.

"No one would imagine, to gaze down on this stream from the rim, that it was such a lively stretch of water," remarked the boy. "It doesn't seem possible."

"Yes, if they had some of this water up on the plateau it would be worth almost its weight in gold," declared Nance. "Water is what Arizona needs and what it has precious little of. Speaking of the danger of the river," continued Nance, "it isn't wholly the water, but the traveling boulders."

"Traveling boulders!" exclaimed the boys.

"Yes. Boulders weighing perhaps a score or more of tons are rolled over and over down the river by the tremendous power of the water, almost with the force and speed of projectiles. Now and again they will run against snags. The water dashing along behind them is suddenly checked under the surface. The result is a great up-wave, such as you have already observed. They are just as likely to go downward or sideways as upward. You never know."

"Then that is the explanation of the cause of those up-waves?" asked the Professor.

"That's the way we figure it out. But we may be wrong. Take an old man's advice and don't monkey with the river."

"I thought you said Dad's beloved Canyon would not hurt him," said Tad teasingly.

"Dad's Canyon won't. The river isn't Dad's The river is a demon. The river would scream with delight were it to get Dad in its cruel clutches," answered the old man thoughtfully, his bristling whiskers drooping to his chest. "Are you boys hungry?"

The boys were. So Dad sought out a comfortable place where they might sit down, a shelf some twenty feet above the edge of the river, whence they could see the turbulent stream for a short distance both ways. It was a wonder to them where all the water came from. The Professor called attention to his former statement that the river drained some three hundred thousand miles of territory. This explanation made the matter clearer to them.

Coffee was made, the ever-ready bacon quickly fried and there in the very heart of the Grand Canyon they ate their midday meal. Never before had they sat down to a meal amid such tremendous forces.

The meal having been finished and Dad having stretched himself out on a rock after his dinner, the boys strolled off along the river, exploring the various crevices.

"Isn't there gold down here?" asked Tad, returning to the shelf.

Dad sat up, stroking his whiskers thoughtfully.

"I reckon you would find tons of it in the pockets of the river if she were to run dry," was the amazing reply.

"But," protested Tad, "is there no way to get it?"

"Not that man knows of. The Almighty, who made the whole business here, is the only one who is engineer enough to get that gold. No, sir, don't have any dreams about getting that gold. It isn't for man, at least not yet. Maybe He to whom it belongs is saving it for some other age, for folks who need it more than we do."

"Nobody ever will need it more than we do," interposed Stacy. "Why, just think, I could buy a whole stable full of horses with what I could get out of one of those pockets."

"Maybe I'll show you where you can pan a little of the yellow out, before you finish your trip."

Later in the day the guide decided that it was time to start for the surface again. But the boys begged to be allowed to remain in the Canyon over night. It was an experience that they felt sure would be worth while. For a wonder, Professor Zepplin sided with them in this request.

"Well, I'll go up and water the stock, then if you want to stay here, why, all right," decided Dad.

"I will go with you," said Tad.

"Professor, I'll leave the rest of the boys in your charge. Don't let them monkey with the river. I don't want to lose anybody this trip. Fall in there, and you'll bring up in the Pacific Ocean -- what's left of you will. Nothing ever'll stop you till you've hit the Sandwich Islands or some other heathen country."

The boys promised and so did the Professor, and both men knew the lads would keep their word, for by this time they held that stream in wholesome respect.

Chunky, after the guide and Tad had left, perched himself on the point of a rock where he lifted up his voice in "Where the Silvery Colorado Wends Its Way," Ned Rector occupying his time by shying rocks at the singer, but Chunky finished his song and had gotten half way through it a second time before one of Ned's missiles reached him. That put an end to the song and brought on a rough and tumble fight in which Ned and Stacy were the sole participants. Chunky, of course, got the worst of it. The two combatants locked arms and strolled away down the river bank after Chunky had been sufficiently punished for trying to sing.

Night in the canyon was an experience. The roaring of the river which no longer could be seen was almost terrifying. Then, too, a strange weird moaning sounded all about them. Dad, who had returned, explained that it was supposed to be the wind. He confided to Tad that it was the spirit of the Canyon uttering its warning.

"Warning of what?"

"I don't know. Maybe a storm. But you can believe something's going to come off, kid," answered Nance with emphasis.

Something did come off. Tad and Nance had fetched the blankets of the party back with them, together with two large bundles of wood for the camp fire, which materials they had let down from point to point at the end of their ropes. Tad had learned always to carry his lasso at his belt. It was the most useful part of his equipment. He had gotten the other boys into the habit of doing the same. Rifles had been left in the camp above, as they were a burden in climbing down the rocks. But all hands carried their heavy revolvers.

A very comfortable camping place was located Under an overhanging shelf of rock, the camp fire just outside lighting up the chamber in a most cheerful manner. There after supper the party sat listening to Dad's stories of the Canyon during some of his thirty years' experience with it.

The wind was plainly rising. It drew the flames of the fire first in one direction, then in another. Nance regarded the signs questioningly. After a little he got up and strolled out to the edge of the roaring river. Tad and Chunky followed him.

"We are going to have a storm," said Dad.

"A heavy one?" asked Tad.

"A regular hummer!"

"Rain?"

"Everything. The whole thing. I'm sorry now that we didn't go back up the trail, but maybe we'd never got up before we were caught. However, we're pretty safe down here, unless --- "

"Unless what?" piped Chunky.

"Unless we get wet," answered Nance, though Tad knew that was not what was in the guide's mind.

Just as they were turning back to the camp there came an explosion that seemed as if the walls of the Canyon had been rent in twain. Chunky uttered a yell and leaped straight up into the air. Tad took firm hold of the fat boy's arm.

"Don't be a fool. That was thunder and lightning. The lightning struck somewhere in the Canyon. Isn't that it, Dad?"

Nance nodded.

"It's always doing that. It's been plugging away at Dad's Canyon for millions of years, but the Canyon is doing business at the same old stand. I hope those pintos are all right up there," added the guide anxiously.

"Mebby they're struck," suggested Stacy.

"Mebby they are," replied Nance. "Come, we'll be getting back unless you want to get wet."

A dash of rain followed almost instantly upon the words. The three started at a trot for the camp. They found the Professor and his two companions anxiously awaiting their return.

"That was a severe bolt," said the Professor.

"Always sounds louder down here, you know," replied Dad. "Echoes."

"Yes, I understand."

"Is -- is it going to rain?" questioned Walter.

"No, it's going to pour," returned Chunky. "You'll need

your rubber boots before long."

"Move that camp fire in further," directed Nance. "It'll be drowned out in a minute."

This was attended with some difficulty, but in a few minutes they had the fire burning brightly under the ledge. Then the rain began. It seemed to be a cloudburst instead of a rain. Lightning was almost incessant, the reports like the bombardment of a thousand batteries of artillery, even the rocks trembling and quaking. Chunky's face grew pale.

"Say, I want to go home," he cried.

"Trot right along. There's nothing to stop ye," answered the guide sarcastically.

"Afraid?" questioned Ned jeeringly.

"No, I'm not afraid. Just scared stiff, that's all," retorted the fat boy.

The shelf of rock that sheltered them had now become the base of a miniature Niagara Falls. The water was pouring over it in tons, making a roaring sound that made that of the river seem faint and far away.

Jim Nance was plainly worried. Tad Butler saw this and so did the Professor, but neither mentioned the fact. Their location was no longer dry. The spray from the waterfall had drenched them to the skin. No one complained. They were too used to hardships.

All at once there came a report louder and different from the others, followed by a crashing, a thundering, a quaking of the rocks beneath their feet, that sent the blood from the face of every man in the party. Even Dad's face grayed ever so little.

The next second each one was thrown violently to the ground. A sound was in their ears as if the universe had blown up.

"We're killed!" howled Chunky.

"Help, help!" yelled Walter Perkins.

"What -- what is it?" roared the Professor.

"We're struck!" shouted Tad.

"Lie still. Hug the wall!" bellowed the stentorian voice of Jim Nance, who himself had crept closer to the Canyon wall and lay hugging it tightly.

The deafening, terrifying reports continued. One corner of the ledge over their heads split off, sending a volley of stones showering over them, leaving the faces of some of the party flecked with blood where the jagged particles had cut into their flesh.

It was a terrible moment for the Pony Rider Boys.

CHAPTER X

ESCAPE IS WHOLLY CUT OFF

Not one could collect his thoughts sufficiently to reason out what had taken place. The guide, however, had known from the first. He feared that his charges would be killed, but there was nothing more that he could do.

The bombarding continued, some explosions sounding near at hand, others further down or up the Canyon, but each of sufficient force to send shivers up and down the spines of the Pony Rider Boys. They never had experienced anything approaching this.

"I'm going to stand up," declared Tad, rising to his feet. "I won't be killed any quicker standing than lying down. Besides, I don't like to shirk."

"Stand up if you want to, but keep close to the wall," ordered Dad, himself rising to his feet.

One by one the boys got up, Professor Zepplin following the example of the guide. They had to shout in speaking in order to make themselves heard above the bombardment, the roaring of the river and the cataract over their heads.

"What is going on up there?" shouted Tad.

"Mountain falling in!"

"I knew it! I knew it!" yelled Chunky. "I knew something would fall down as soon as I got here."

No one laughed. The situation was too serious for laughter.

"Is it a land or a rock slide?" questioned Tad further.

"Both," shouted Nance. "Mostly boulders."

The rain has loosened them and they are raining down on us. We're lucky we had this shelf to get under."

"From the present outlook I am afraid the shelf isn't going to protect us much longer," said Tad.

"Keep close to the wall and you will be all right. It won't break off short up to the wall. I've seen rock slides, but never anything quite like this. You see, the spirit of the Canyon was right," nodded Nance.

"Spirits? What spirits?" demanded Chunky. "Is this place haunted? Don't tell me it is. Haven't I got enough to worry me already without being chased by ghosts?

"Chased by goats?" shouted the Professor.

"Who said anything about goats?" retorted Stacy. "I said g-h-o-s-t-s, spooks, spookees or spookors or whatever you've a mind to call them."

"Oh, I hope you are not losing your mind, Stacy."

"Might as well lose my mind as to lose my life. Mind wouldn't be any use to me after I was dead, would it?"

"The storm is dying out," called Ned.

Tad started to step from under the shelf, Nance grasped and hauled him back. Just then a great boulder, weighing many tons, struck the rock just above their heads, then bounded off into the river, which it struck with a mighty splash. The contact with the rocks sent off a shower of sparks, a perfect rain of them.

"I -- I guess I need a guardian," said the lad rather weakly.

"Yes, you probably would have been killed by the smaller pieces that broke off," answered Nance. "Be content to stay where you are."

"How long have we got to stay cooped up in this half cave?" demanded Stacy.

"All night, maybe," answered Dad.

"Good night!" said the fat boy, Slipping down until he had assumed a sitting posture. He lay down and was asleep in a short time. Stacy woke with a start when another giant rock smote the wall just above their cave, exploding into thousands of pieces from the violent contact.

"Stop that noise! How do you suppose a fellow's going to sleep when --- "

Stacy struggled slowly to his feet when he saw the drawn faces of his companions.

"Was that another of them?" he asked hesitatingly.

"Yes," answered Tad, with a nod. "It is grand, but terrible."

"I don't see anything grand about it. I guess I won't lie down again. I never can sleep any more after being awakened from my first nap," declared the fat boy.

No one slept for the rest of the night. The bombardment continued at intervals all through the black, terrifying night. The Colorado, into which billions of gallons of water had been dumped, was rising rapidly, an angry, threatening flood.

"Is there any danger of the river overflowing on us?" asked Professor Zepplin.

"No. No single night's rain would do it. The rain is pretty nearly ended now, as you can see for yourself. But there's no telling how long those fellows will continue to roll down. I've seen the same thing before, but this is the worst," declared Dad.

"All on account of the Pony Rider Boys," piped Stacy. "Miss Nature is determined to give us our money's worth in experience. I've had mine already. She can't quit any too soon to suit me."

After a time the guide crept out, his ears keyed sharply to catch warning sounds from above. Nance had been out but a moment when he darted back under the protecting ledge. He was just in time. A giant boulder struck the earth right in front of their place of refuge. From that moment on no one ventured out. About an hour before daylight, the storm having lulled, the failing boulders coming down with less frequency, all hands sank down on their wet blankets one by one, and dropped off to sleep.

When they awakened the day had dawned. The sun was glowing on the peaks of Pluto Pyramid and the Algonkin Terraces far above them on the opposite side of the gorge. Tad Butler was the first to open his eyes that morning. He sprang up with a shout.

"Sleepy heads! Turn out!"

Dad was on his feet with a bound. Then came the Professor, Ned and Walter in the order named, with Stacy Brown limping along painfully at the rear.

"How do you feel this fine morning?" glowed Tad, nodding at Stacy.

"I? Oh, I'm all bunged up. How's the weather?"

"Nature is smiling," answered Tad.

"All right. As long as she doesn't grin, I won't kick. If she grins I'm blest if I'll stand for it."

"Whose turn is it to get breakfast?" questioned Ned.

"What little there is to get I will attend to," said Tad. "We are long on experience but short on food."

Still, breakfast was a cheerful meal, even though all were still wet, their muscles stiffened from sleeping in puddles, from which they were obliged to dip the water for their coffee. They enjoyed the meal just as much as if it had been a banquet, however.

Dad's face did not reflect the general joy that was apparent on the faces of the others. Tad observed this, but made no comment. Finally Stacy Brown discovered something of the sort, too.

"Dad, you've got a grouch on this lovely morning," said Stacy.

"No, I never have a grouch."

"Your whiskers are rising. I thought you had."

"I'd rather have my whiskers standing out some of the time than to have my tongue hanging out all of the time," replied the guide witheringly.

"I guess that will be about all for you, Chunky," jeered Ned.

"Do we start as soon as we have finished here?" asked the Professor of Nance.

"We do not," was the brief reply.

"May I ask why not?"

"Because we can't start."

"Can't?" wondered Professor Zepplin.

Tad saw that something was wrong. What that something was he had not the remotest idea.

"No, we won't go up Bright Angel Trail to-day."

"Why not? Why won't we?" piped Stacy.

"Because there isn't any Bright Angel Trail to go up," returned the guide grimly. "The bad place in the trail was all torn out by the ripping boulders last night. Nothing short of a bird could make its way over that stretch of trail now."

"Then what are we going to do?" cried the Professor.

"Do? We're going to stay here. Escape is for the present wholly cut off --- "

"Can't we climb up a trail lower down?" asked Ned.

"Ain't no trail this side of the wall by the river, and the river is just as bad as the wall. I reckon we'll stay here for a time at least."

The Pony Rider Boys looked at each other solemnly. Theirs was, indeed, a serious predicament, much more so than they realized.

CHAPTER XI

A TRYING TIME

For a moment following the announcement no one spoke.

The Professor gazed straight into the stern face of the guide, whose whiskers were still drooping.

"We are prisoners here? Is that it, Nance?" stammered Professor Zepplin.

"That's about it, I reckon. The trail's busted. There ain't no other way to get out that I know of and I reckon I know these canyons pretty well."

"Then what shall we do?"

"Well, I reckon we'll wait till somebody misses us and comes down after us."

"Oh, well, they will do that this morning. Of course they will miss us," declared the Professor, as if the matter were entirely settled.

The expression on Dad's face plainly showed that he was not quite so confident as was the Professor. There was one factor that Professor Zepplin had not taken into consideration. Food! There was barely enough left for a meal for one person. Dad surmised this, so he asked Tad just how much food they had left.

"Our supply," said Tad, "consists of three biscuit, one orange and two lemons."

The boys groaned.

"I'll take the biscuit. You can have the rest," was Chunky's liberal offer. "How about it?"

"You will get a lemon handed to you at twelve o'clock noon to-day,"jeered Ned Rector.

"Then I'll pass it along to the one who needs it the most," retorted Stacy quickly.

"The question is," said the Professor, "is there nothing that we can do to attract the attention of others?"

"I have been thinking of that," answered Nance. "I wish now that we had brought our rifles."

"Why?"

"To shoot and attract attention of whoever may be on the rim."

"We might shoot our revolvers," suggested Tad.

"We will do that. It is doubtful if the reports can be heard above, and even then I am doubtful about any of the tenderfeet understanding what the shots mean. About our only hope is that some one who knows will come down the trail. They won't go further than the

Gardens, but finding our mustangs there a mountaineer would understand."

"Shall I take a shot?" asked Walter.

"Yes."

Walter fired five shots into the river. After an interval Chunky let go five more. This continued until each had fired a round of five shots. After each round they listened for an answering shot from above, but none came. Thus matters continued until noon, when the remaining food was distributed among the party.

"This is worse than nothing," cried Chunky. "This excites my appetite. If you see me frothing at the mouth don't think I've got a dog bite. That's my appetite fighting with my stomach. I'll bet my gun that the appetite wins too."

The day wore away slowly. Tad made frequent trips down the river as far as he could get before being stopped by a great wall of rock that rose abruptly for nearly a thousand feet above him. He gazed up this glittering expanse of rock until his neck ached, then he went back to camp. An idea was working in Tad's mind, but it was as yet undeveloped.

At intervals the shots were tried again, though no reply followed. Night came on. Before dark Dad had gathered some driftwood that he found in crevices of the rocks. The wood was almost bone dry and a crackling, cheerful fire was soon burning.

"If we only had something to eat now, we'd be all right," said Walter mournfully.

"You want something to eat?" questioned Chunky.

"I should say I do."

"Oh, well, that's easily fixed."

Stacy stepped over to a rock, made a motion as if ringing a telephone bell, then listened.

"Hello! hello! Is that the hotel, El Tovar Hotel? Very well; this is Brown. Brown! Yes. Well, we want you to send out dinner for six. Six! Can't you understand plain English? Yes, six. Oh, well, I think we'll have some porter house steak smothered in onions. Smothered! We'll have some corn cakes and honey, some--some -- um -- some baked potatoes, about four quarts of strawberries. And by the way, got any apple pie? Yes? Well, you might send down a half dozen pies and --- "

Chunky got no further. With a howl, Ned Rector, Tad Butler and Walter Perkins made a concerted rush for him.

Ned fell upon the unfortunate fat boy first. Stacy went down in a heap with Ned jamming his head into the dirt that had been washed up by the river at flood time. A moment more and Ned was at the bottom of the heap with Stacy, the other two boys having piled on top.

"Here, here!" shouted the Professor.

"Let 'em scrap," grinned Dad. "They'll forget they're hungry."

They did. After the heap had been unpiled, the boys

got up, their clothes considerably the worse for the conflict, their faces red, but smiling and their spirits considerably higher.

"You'll get worse than that if you tantalize us in that way again," warned Tad. "We can stand for your harmless jokes, but this is cruel --- "

" -- ty to animals," finished Chunky.

"What you'll get will make you sure of that."

"Come over here and get warm, Brown," called the guide.

"Oh, he's warmed sufficiently," laughed Tad. "We have attended to that. He won't get chills to-night, I promise you."

Breathing hard, their eyes glowing, the boys squatted down around the camp fire. No sooner had they done so than a thrilling roar sounded off somewhere in a canyon to their right, the roar echoing from rock to rock, from canyon to canyon, dying away in the far distance.

"For goodness' sake, what is that?" gasped Stacy.

"Mountain lion," answered the guide shortly.

"Can -- can he get here?" stammered Walter.

"He can if he wants to."

"I -- I hope he changes his mind if he does want to," breathed Stacy.

"I wish we had our rifles," muttered Ned.

"What for?" demanded Dad.

"To shoot lions, of course."

"Humph!"

"Couldn't we have a lion hunt while we are out here?" asked Tad enthusiastically.

"You could if the lion didn't hunt you."

"Wouldn't that be great, fellows?" cried Tad. "The Pony Rider Boys as lion hunters."

"Great," chorused the boys. "When shall it be?" added Ned.

"It won't be till after we get out of this hole," declared Dad. "And from present indications, that won't be to-night."

"Tell us something about the lions," urged Walter. "Are they ugly?"

"Well, they ain't exactly household pets," answered the guide, with a faint smile.

"Is it permitted to hunt them?" interjected the Professor.

"Yes, there's no law against it. The lions kill the deer and the government is glad to be rid of the lions. But you won't get enough of them to cause a flurry in the lion market."

"No, there's more probability of there being a panic in the Pony Rider market," chuckled Tad.

"I'm not afraid," cried Stacy.

"No, Chunky isn't afraid," jeered Ned. "He doesn't want to go home when the marbles roll down from the mountain! Oh, no, he isn't afraid! He's just looking for dangerous sport."

Their repartee was interrupted by another roar, louder than the first. But though they listened for a long time there was no repetition of the disturbing roar of the king of the canyons.

Soon after that the lads went to bed. Tonight they slept soundly, for they had had little sleep the previous night, as the reader knows. When they awakened on the following morning the conditions had not changed. They were still prisoners in the Grand Canyon not far from the foot of Bright Angel Trail. All hands awoke to the consciousness that unless something were done, and at once, they would find themselves face to face with starvation. It was not a cheerful prospect.

There was no breakfast that morning, though Chunky, who had picked up a cast-away piece of orange peel, was munching it with great satisfaction, rolling his eyes from one to the other of his companions.

"Don't. You might excite your appetite again," warned Ned.

Tad, who had been out for another exploring tour

along the river, had returned, walking briskly.

"Well, did you find a trail?" demanded Chunky.

"No, but I have found a way out of this hole," answered Tad, with emphasis.

"What?" exclaimed Dad, whirling on him almost savagely.

"Yes, I have found a way. I'm going to carry out a plan and I promise that with good luck I'll get you all out of here safely. I shall need some help, but the thing can be done, I know."

"What is your plan?" asked the Professor.

"I'll tell you," said Tad. "But don't interrupt me, please, until I have finished."

CHAPTER XII

BRAVING THE ROARING COLORADO

The Pony Riders drew closer, Dad leaned against the rocky wall of the Canyon, while the Professor peered anxiously into the lad's face.

"I'll bet it's a crazy plan," muttered Stacy.

"We will hear what you have to say and decide upon its feasibility afterwards," announced the Professor.

"Mr.Nance, if a man were below the horseshoe down the Canyon there, he would be able to make his way over to the Bright Angel Trail, would he not?"

"Yes. A fellow who knew how to climb among the rocks could make it."

"He could get right over on our own trail, could he not?"

"Sure! But what good would that do us?"

"Couldn't he let down ropes and get us out?"

"I reckon he could at that."

"You don't think we are going to be discovered here until perhaps it is too late, do you, Mr.Nance?"

"We always have hopes. There being nothing we can do, the only thing for us is to sit down and hope."

"And starve? No, thank you. Not for mine!"

"Nor mine. It's time we men did something," declared Stacy pompously.

"As I have had occasion to remark before, children should be seen and not heard," asserted Ned Rector.

"Kindly be quiet. We are listening to Master Tad," rebuked the Professor. "Go ahead, Tad."

"There isn't much to say, except that I propose to get on the other side of the horseshoe and climb back over the rocks to our trail. If I am fortunate enough to get there the rest will be easy and I'll have you up in a short time. How about it, Dad?" asked the boy lightly, as if his proposal were nothing out of the ordinary.

Dad took a few steps forward.

"How do ye propose to get across that stretch of water there to reach the other side of the horseshoe?"

"Swim it, of course."

The guide laughed harshly.

"Swim it? Why, kid a boat wouldn't live in that boiling pot for two minutes. What could a mere man hope to do against that demon?"

"It is my opinion that a man would do better for a few moments against the water than a boat would. I think I can do it."

"No, if anybody does that kind of a trick it will be Jim Nance."

"Do you swim?"

"Like a chunk of marble. Living on the plains all a fellow's life doesn't usually make a swimmer of him."

"I thought so. That makes me all the more determined to do this thing."

"Somebody hold me or I'll be doing it myself," cried Chunky.

No one paid any attention to the fat boy's remark.

"I can't permit it, Tad," said the Professor, with an emphatic shake of the head. "No, you could never make it. It would be suicide."

"I'm going to try it," insisted the Pony Rider.

"You most certainly are not."

"But there is little danger. Don't you see I should be floating down with the current. Almost before I knew it I should be on the other side of the horseshoe there. Besides you would have hold of the rope."

"Rope?" demanded Dad.

"Yes, of course."

"Where are you going to get ropes? They're all up there on the mountainside."

"We still have our lassoes."

"Explain. I don't understand," urged Professor Zepplin.

"It is my plan to tie the lassoes together. We have six of them. That will make nearly two hundred feet. One or two of you can take hold of the free end of the rope, the other end being about my waist. In case I should be carried away from the shore, why all you have to do will be to haul me back. Isn't that a simple proposition?"

"It's a crazy one," nodded the Professor.

"Come to think it over, I believe it could be done," reflected Nance. "If I could swim at all I'd do it myself, but I'd drown inside of thirty seconds after I stepped a foot in the water. Why, I nearly drown every time I wash for breakfast."

Stacy was about to make a remark, but checked himself. It was evidently not a seemly remark. It must have been more than ordinarily flippant to have caused Chunky to restrain himself.

"I move we let Tad try it, Professor," proposed Ned.

"I don't approve of it at all. No, sir, I most emphatically do not."

"But surely, Professor, there can be no danger in it at all. It is very simple," urged young Butler.

Tad knew better. It was not a simple thing to do. It was distinctly a perilous, if not a foolhardy feat. Nance knew this, too, but he had grown to feel a great confidence in Tad Butler. He believed that if anyone could brave those swirling waters and come out alive, that one was Tad Butler. But it was a desperate chance. Still, with the rope tied around the lad's waist, it was as the boy had said, they could haul him back quickly.

"Professor, I am in favor of letting him try it if he is a good swimmer," announced the guide.

"Pshaw, you couldn't drown Tad," declared Ned.

"No, you couldn't drown Tad," echoed Chunky. "Not any more than you could drown me."

"Perhaps you would like to try it yourself?" grinned Nance.

"Yes, I can hardly hold myself. I am afraid every minute that I'll jump right into that raging flood there and strike out for the other side of the horseshoe," returned Stacy, striking a diving attitude.

They laughed, but as quickly sobered. Tad was already at work making firm splices in the two ropes that he held in his hand.

"Pass over your ropes, boys. We have no time to lose. The river is getting higher every minute now, and there's no telling what condition it will be in an hour from now."

The others passed over their ropes, some willingly enough, others with reluctance. Tad spliced them together, tested each knot with all his strength and nodded his approval.

"I guess they will hold now," he said, stripping off his coat after having thrown his hat aside and tossed off his cartridge belt and revolver.

"Walt, you take care of those things for me, please, and in case I get you folks out, fetch them up with you."

Walter Perkins nodded as he picked up the belongings of his chum.

"Mr.Nance," said Tad, "I think you and Ned are the strongest, so I'll ask you two to take hold of the rope when I get started. If you need help the Professor will lend a hand."

Professor Zepplin shook his head. He did not approve of this at all. However, it seemed their only hope. Tad started for the lower end of the walled-in enclosure, the others following him. The lad made the rope fast around his waist, twisting it about so that the knot was on the small of his back. Thus the rope would not interfere with his swimming. He then uncoiled the rope, stretching it along the ground to make sure that there were no kinks in it.

"There, everything appears to be in working order. Don't you envy me my fine swim, boys?" Tad laughed cheerfully.

"Yes, we do," chorused the boys.

It must not be thought that Tad Butler did not fully realize the peril into which he was so willingly going.

He knew there was a big chance against his ever making his goal, but he was willing to take the slender remaining chance that he might make it.

"All ready," he said coolly.

Dad and Ned took hold of the rope.

"Don't hold on to it at all unless I shout to you to do so. I must be left free. Let me be the judge if I am to be hauled back or not."

With a final glance behind, to see that all was in readiness, Tad stepped to the edge of the water. Chunky pressed up close to him.

"Is there any last request that you want me to make to relatives or friends, Tad?" asked the fat boy solemnly.

"Tell them to be good to my Chunky, for he's such a tender plant that he will perish unless he has the most loving care. Here I go!"

With a wave of his hand, Tad plunged into the swirling waters. Though his plunge was seen, the sound of it was borne down by the thunderous roar of the river. As Butler vanished it was as though he had gone to his instant doom.

Instinctively the two men holding the rope tightened their grip, beginning to haul in. But Tad's head showed and they eased off again.

Just a few moments more, and Tad was seized by the waters and hurled up into the air.

"He jumps like a bass," chuckled Chunky.

"Quit that talk!" ordered Ned sharply. "Poor Tad, we've let him go to a hopeless death!"

All watched Tad breathlessly -- whenever they could see him. More often the boy was invisible to those on land.

A strong swimmer, and an intelligent one, Tad had more than found his match in these angry, cruel waters. Though the current was in the direction that he wanted to go, the eddies seemed bent on dragging him out to the middle of the stream, where he must be most helpless of all.

Tad was fighting with all the strength that remained to him when an up-wave met him, caught him and hurled him back fully ten feet. Butler now found his feet entangled in the rope.

"He's having a fearful battle!" gasped Walter, whose face had gone deathly pale.

Professor Zepplin nodded, unable to speak. By a triumph of strength, backed by his cool head and keen judgment, Tad brought himself out of this dangerous pocket of water, only to meet others. His strength seemed to be failing now.

"Haul him back!" ordered the Professor hoarsely. "Haul him back!"

They tried, but at that moment the rope parted -- sawed in two over a sharp edge of rock!

CHAPTER XIII

A BATTLE MIGHTILY WAGED

The land end of the rope fell limp in the hands of Jim Nance and Ned Rector.

"It's gone -- gone!" wailed Ned.

"That settles him," answered the guide in a hopeless tone.

"Oh, he's lost, he's lost!" cried Walter. "Can no one do anything?"

Chunky, with sudden determination, threw off his coat, and started on a run for the river. Dodging the Professor's outstretched hands, Chunky sprang into the water.

With a roar Dad hurled the rope toward the fat boy. The guide had no time in which to fashion a loop, but he had thrown the rope doubled. Fortunately the coil caught Chunky's right foot and the lad was hauled back feet first, choking, half drowned, his head being dragged under water despite his struggles to get free.

The instant they hauled him to the bank the Professor seized the lad and began shaking him.

"Leggo! Lemme go, I tell you. I'm going after Tad!"

Stacy Brown was terribly in earnest this time. He was fighting mad because they had pulled him back from what would have been sure death to him. They had never given Stacy credit for such pluck, and Ned and Walter gazed at him with new interest in their eyes. It was necessary to hold the fat boy. He was still struggling, determined to go to Tad's rescue.

In the meantime their attention had been drawn from Tad for the moment. When they looked again they failed to find him.

"There he is," shouted Ned, as the boy was seen to rise from the water and plunge head foremost into it again. Tad did not appear to be fighting now.

"He's helpless! He's hurt!" cried the Professor.

"I reckon that's about the end of the lad," answered Nance in a low tone. "There's nothing we can do but to wait."

"I see him again!" shouted Walter.

They could see the lad being tumbled this way and that, hurled first away from the shore, then on toward it. Nance was regarding the buffeted Pony Rider keenly. He saw that Tad was really nearing the shore, but that he was helpless.

"What has happened to him?" demanded the Professor hoarsely. "Is he drowned?"

"It's my opinion that he has been banged against a rock

and knocked out. I can't tell what'll be the end of it, but it looks mighty bad. There he goes, high and dry!" fairly screamed Dad, while his whiskers tilted upwards at a sharp angle.

Tad had been hurled clear of the water, hurled to the dry rocks on which he had been flung as if the river wanted no more of him. The watchers began to shout. They danced about almost beside themselves with anxiety. No one could go to Tad's assistance, if, indeed, he were not beyond assistance.

A full twenty minutes of this nerve-racking anxiety had passed when Dad thought he saw a movement of Tad's form. A few moments later the boy was seen to struggle to a sitting posture, where he sat for a short time, both hands supporting his head.

Such a yell as the Pony Rider Boys uttered might have been heard clear up on the rim of the Grand Canyon had there been any one there to hear it. Dad danced a wild hornpipe, the Professor strode up and down, first thrusting his hands into his pockets, then withdrawing and waving them above his head. Stacy had settled down on the rocks with the tears streaming down his cheeks. Stacy wasn't joking now. This emotion was real.

They began to shout out Tad's name. It was plain that he heard them, for he waved a listless hand then returned to his former position.

"That boy is all iron," breathed the admiring guide.

The noise of the river was so great that they could not ask him if he were hurt seriously. But Tad answered the question himself a few minutes later by getting up. He stood for a moment swaying as if he would fall over again, then staggered to the wall, against which he leaned, still holding his head.

"He must have got an awful wallop," declared Dad.

Shortly after that Tad appeared to have recovered somewhat, for he was seen to be gazing up over the rocks, apparently trying to choose a route for himself.

"How can he ever make that dizzy climb in his condition?" groaned the Professor.

"We'll see. I think he can do anything," returned Nance.

Tad walked back and forth a few times, exercising his muscles, then turned toward the rocks which he began to climb. He proceeded slowly and with great caution, evidently realizing the peril of his undertaking, but taking no greater chances than he was obliged to do.

Little by little he worked his way upward, Now and then halting, clinging to the rocks for support while he rested. After a time he looked down at his companions. Nance waved a hand, signaling Tad to turn to the right. Tad saw and understood the signal and acted accordingly.

Once he stood up and gazed off over the rugged peaks, sharp knife-like edges and sheer wails before him. There seemed not sufficient foothold for a bird where he was standing, and though a thousand feet above the river, he seemed not to feel the height at all nor to be in the least dizzy.

It was dangerous work, exhausting work; but oh! what self-reliance, what pluck and levelheadedness was Tad Butler displaying. Had he never accomplished anything worth while in his life, those who saw him now could but admire the lad's wonderful courage.

They hung upon his movements, scarcely breathing at all, as little by little the lad crept along, now swinging by his hands from one ledge to another, now creeping around a sharp bend on hand and knees, now hanging with nothing more secure than thin air underneath him, with face flattened against a rock, resting. It was a sight to thrill and to make even strong men shiver.

For a long time Tad disappeared from view. The watchers did not know where he had gone, but Nance explained that he had crept around the opposite side of the butte where he had last been seen, hoping to discover better going there, which Jim was of the opinion he would find.

This proved to be the case when after what seemed an interminable time, the Pony Rider once more appeared, creeping steadily on toward the trail above the broken spot.

This went on for the greater part of two hours.

"He's safe. Thank God!" cried the guide.

The Pony Rider Boys whooped.

"You stay here!" directed the guide. Nance began clambering up the rocky trail to a point from which he would be able to talk to the boy. Arriving at this spot,

Dad waited. At last Tad appeared, dragging himself along.

"Good boy! Fine boy! Dad's Canyon is proud of you, boy!"

Tad sank down, shaking his head, breathing hard, as the guide could see, even at that distance. After a time Tad recovered his wind sufficiently to be able to talk.

"What happened to you?" called Dad.

"I got a bump. I don't really know what did occur. The ropes are all washed away, Dad. I don't know how I'm going to help you up here now that I have got up. Aren't there any vines of which I could make a ladder?"

"Nary a vine that'll make a seventy-five-foot ladder."

"Then there is only one thing for me to do."

"What's that?"

"Hurry to the rim and get ropes."

"I reckon you'll have to do that, kid, if you think you're able. Are you much knocked out?"

"I'm all right. Tell them not to worry. I may be gone some time, but I shall be back."

"Good luck! I wish I could help you."

"I don't need help now. There is no further danger. Are my friends down there hungry?"

"Stacy Brown is thinking of nibbling rocks."

Tad laughed, then began climbing up the trail. Nance, watching him narrowly, saw that the boy was very weary, being scarcely able to drag himself along. After a time Tad passed out of sight up what was left of Bright Angel Trail. Nance, with a sigh, turned to begin retracing his steps down to the Pony Rider Boys' party.

"Well, he made it, didn't he?" cried Ned. "We have been watching him all the time."

"There's a real man," answered the guide, with an emphatic nod. "Pity there aren't more like him."

"There is one like him," spoke up Chunky.

"Who?"

"Little me," answered the fat boy, tapping his chest modestly.

"That's so; Chunky did jump into the raging flood," said Walter. "We mustn't forget that he acted the part of a brave man while we were standing there shivering and almost gasping for breath."

"Brave?" drawled Ned sarcastically.

"Ned Rector, you know you were scared stiff," retorted Walter.

"Well, I'll be honest with you, I was. Who wouldn't have been? Even the Professor's mustache changed color for the moment."

The afternoon passed. It was now growing dark, for the night came on early down there in the Canyon. On the tops of the peaks the lowering sun was lighting up the red sandstone, making it appear like a great flame on the polished walls.

"Isn't it time Tad were getting back?" asked the Professor anxiously.

"Well, it's a long, hard climb, you know. All of seven miles the way one has to go. That makes fourteen miles up and back, and they're real miles, as you know."

"I hope nothing has happened to the boy."

"Leave it to him. He knows how to take care of himself."

No one thought of lying down to sleep. In the first place, all were too hungry. Then, again, at any moment Tad might return. Midnight arrived. Suddenly Nance held up his hands for silence.

"Whoo-oo!"

It was a long-drawn, far-away call.

"That's Tad," said Nance. "We'd better gather up our belongings and get up to the break in the trail."

The guide answered the call by a similar "whoo-oo," after which all began climbing cautiously. In the darkness it was dangerous business, but a torch held in the hands of Jim Nance aided them materially. Far up on the side of the Canyon they could see three flickering points of light.

"It's the kid. He's got somebody with him. I thought he'd do that. He's a wise one," chuckled the guide.

The climb was made in safety. The party ar rived at the base at last, the boys shouting joyously as they saw Tad waving a torch at them. At least they supposed it was Tad.

"What do you think about waiting until daylight for the climb?" shouted Butler.

"I'll see what they say," answered Nance. "What about it, gentlemen?"

"I think it perhaps would be safer." This from the Professor.

"What, spend another night in this hole?" demanded Stacy. "No, sirree."

"Please let us go on up, Professor," begged Walter.

"Yes, we don't want to stay down here. We can climb at night as well as in daylight," urged Chunky.

"What have you got, ropes?" called Nance.

"I've brought down some rope ladders, which I have spliced --- "

"I hope you've done a better job on the splicing than you did on your own rope when you sailed across the horseshoe bend," shouted Stacy.

"If you haven't, I refuse to trust my precious life to your old rope."

"Too bad about your precious life," laughed Ned. "Well, Professor, what do you say?"

"Is it safe, Nance?"

"As safe now as at any other time."

"All right."

"Let down your ladder," called the guide. "Be sure that it is well secured. How many have you with you?"

"Three men, if that is what you mean."

"Very good."

The rope ladder was let down. Those below were just able to reach it with their hands. It came within less than a foot of being too short.

"Who is going up first?" asked the guide.

"The Professor, of course," replied Chunky magnanimously.

"That is very thoughtful of you, Stacy," smiled Professor Zepplin.

"Yes, you are the heaviest. If the rope doesn't break with you, it's safe for the rest of us," answered Chunky, whereat there was a general laugh.

"Very good, young man. I will accommodate you,"

announced the Professor grimly, grasping the rope and pulling himself up with the assistance of Nance and the boys.

The rope swayed dizzily.

"Hold it there!" shouted the Professor.

Nance had already grasped the end of the ladder and was holding to it with his full weight. After a long time a shout from above told them that Professor Zepplin had arrived safely at the top. Walter went up next, then Chunky and Ned, followed finally by Jim Nance himself after their belongings had been hauled to the top.

Professor Zepplin embraced Tad immediately upon reaching the trail above. The boys joked Butler about being such a poor swimmer. About that time they discovered that Tad had a gash nearly four inches long on his head where he had come in contact with the sharp edge of a rock in the river. Tad had lost much blood and was still weak and pale from his terrific experiences. Nance wrung Tad Butler's hand until Tad winced.

"Ain't a man in the whole Grand who could have done what you did, youngster," declared Dad enthusiastically.

"The question is, did you fetch down anything to eat?" demanded Chunky.

"Yes, of course I did."

"Where is it? Lead me to it," shouted the fat boy.

"I left the stuff up at the Garden, where the mustangs are. We will go up there, the Professor and Mr.Nance approving."

The Professor and Mr.Nance most certainly did approve of the suggestion, for both were very hungry. The men who had come down with Tad led the way with their torches. It was a long, hard climb, the use of the ropes being found necessary here and there for convenience and to save time. Tad had had none of these conveniences when he went up. How he had made the trip so easily as he appeared to make it set the boys to wondering.

Baskets of food were found at the Garden. The party did full justice to the edibles, then, acting on the suggestion of Nance, they rolled up in their blankets and went to sleep. First, however, Professor Zepplin had examined the wound in Tad's head. He found it a scalp wound. The Professor washed and dressed the wound, after which Tad went to bed.

On the following morning they mounted their mustangs and started slowly for the rim, where they arrived some time after noon. The Pony Rider Boys instantly went into camp near the hotel, for it had been decided to take a full day's rest before starting out on the long trip. This time they were to take their pack train with them and cut off from civilization for the coming few weeks, they would live in the Canyon, foraging for what food they were unable to carry with them.

The guests at the hotel, after hearing of Tad Butler's bravery, tried to make a hero of the lad, but Tad would have none of it. He grew red in the face every time anyone suggested that he had done anything out of the ordinary. And deep down in his heart the lad did not believe that he had. Professor Zepplin, however, called a surgeon, who took five stitches in the scalp wound.

On the following morning camp was struck and the party started out for Bright Angel Gulch and Cataract Canyon, in both of which places some interesting as well as exciting experiences awaited them. Nance had brought three of his hunting dogs with him in case any game were started.

The boys were looking forward to shooting a lion, though, there being no snow on the ground, it would be difficult for the dogs to strike and follow a trail. How well they succeeded we shall see.

CHAPTER XIV

THE DOGS PICK UP A TRAIL

The man in charge of the pack train having deserted them before the travelers got back from the rim, Dad picked up a half breed whom the boys named Chow, because he was always chewing. If not food, Chow was forever munching on a leaf or a twig or a stick. His jaws were ever at work until the boys were working their own jaws out of pure sympathy.

The march was taken up to Bass Trail, which they reached about noon of the second day and started down. No unusual incident occurred during this journey. They found the trail in good condition, and though steep and precipitous in places, it gave the Pony Rider Boys no worry. After having experienced the perils of the other trail, this one seemed tame.

From Bass Trail they worked their way down and across into Bright Angel Gulch, where they made camp and awaited the arrival of Chow and the mules with their tents and provisions.

Chow arrived late the same day. Tents were pitched and settled. It was decided for the present to make this point their base of supplies. When on short journeys they would travel light, carrying such equipment as was absolutely necessary, and no more.

This gulch was far from the beaten track of the ordinary explorer, a vast but attractive gash in the plateau. In spots there was verdure, and, where the water courses reached in, stretches of grass with here and there patches of gramma grass, grease wood and creosote plants with a profusion of flowers, mostly red, in harmony with the prevailing color of the rocks that towered high above them. At this point the walls of the Canyon reached nearly seven thousand feet up into the air.

Down there on the levels the sun glared fiercely at midday, but along toward night refreshing breezes drifted through the Canyon, making the evenings cool and delightful. But there were drawbacks. There were snakes and insects in this almost tropical lower land. The boys were not greatly disturbed over these things. By this time they were pretty familiar with insects and reptiles, for it will be remembered that they had spent much time in the wilder places of their native country.

For the first twenty-four hours of their stay in "Camp Butler," as they had named their base in honor of Tad himself, they did little more than make short excursions out into the adjoining canyons. The Professor embraced the opportunity to indulge in some scientific researches into the geology of the Canyon, on which in the evening he was wont to dwell at length in language that none of the boys understood. But they listened patiently, for they were very fond of this grizzled old traveler who had now been their companion for so long.

The third night the dogs appeared restless. They lay at

the end of their leashes growling and whipping their tails angrily.

"What is the matter with the dogs?" demanded Tad Butler.

"I think they must have fleas," decided Chunky wisely.

"No, it isn't fleas," said Dad, who had been observing them for the past few minutes. "It's my opinion that there's game hereabouts."

"Deer?" questioned Ned.

"No. More likely it's something that is after the deer."

"Lions?" asked Tad.

"I reckon."

"Have you seen any signs of them?"

"What you might call a sign," Nance nodded. "I found, up in Mystic Canyon this afternoon, all that was left of a deer. The lions had killed it and stripped all the best flesh from the deer. So it's plain enough that the cats are hanging around. I thought we'd come up with some of them down here."

"Wow for the king of beasts!" shouted Chunky, throwing up his sombrero.

"Nothing like a king," retorted Jim Nance. "The mountain lion isn't in any class with African lions. The lion hereabouts is only a part as big. A king -- this mountain lion of ours? You'd better call the beast a dirty savage, and be satisfied with that."

"But we're going to go after some of them, aren't we?" asked Ned.

"Surely," nodded Nance.

"When?" pressed Walter.

"Is it safe?" the more prudent Professor Zepplin wanted to know.

"Safe?" repeated Jim Nance. "Well, when it comes to that, nothing down in this country can be called exactly safe. All sorts of trouble can be had around here for the asking. But I reckon that these young gentlemen will know pretty well how to keep themselves reasonably safe -- all except Mr.Brown, who'll bear some watching."

Even long after they had turned in that night the boys kept on talking about the coming hunts of the next few days. They fairly dreamed lions. In the morning the hunt was the first thing they thought of as they ran to wash up for breakfast. In the near distance could be heard the baying of hounds, for Dad's dogs were no longer chained up.

"I let the dogs loose," Nance explained, noting the eager, questioning glances. "The dogs have got track of something. Hustle your breakfasts! We'll get away with speed."

Breakfast was disposed of in a hurry that morning. Then the boys hustled to get ready for the day's sport. When, a few minutes later, they set off on their ponies, with rifles thrust in saddle boots, revolvers bristling from their belts, ropes looped over the pommels of their saddles, the Pony Rider Boys presented quite a warlike appearance.

"If you were half as fierce as you look I'd run," declared Dad, with a grin.

"Which way do we go?" questioned the Professor.

"We'll all hike up into the Mystic Canyon. There we'll spread out, each man for himself. One of us can't help but fall to the trail of a beast if he is careful."

After reaching the Mystic they heard the dogs in a canyon some distance away. Ned and Walter were sent off to the left, Tad to the north, while the rest remained in the Mystic Canyon to wait there, where the chase should lead at some time during the day.

"Three shots are a signal to come in, or to come to the fellow who shoots," announced the guide. "Look out for yourselves."

Silence soon settled down over Mystic Canyon. Chunky was disappointed that he had not been assigned to go out with one of his companions, he found time hanging heavily on his hands with Nance and the Professor, but he uttered no complaint.

The Professor and guide had dismounted from their ponies and were seated on a rock busily engaged in conversation. Chunky, after glancing at them narrowly, shouldered his rifle and strolled off, leaving his pony tethered to a sapling.

He walked further than he had intended, making his way to a rise of ground about a quarter of a mile away, with the hope that he might catch a glimpse of some of his companions. Once on the rise, which was quite heavily wooded, he seemed to hear the hounds much more plainly than before. It seemed to Stacy that they were approaching from the other side, opposite to that which the rest were watching. He glanced down into the canyon, but could see neither of the two older men.

"Most exciting chase I've ever been in," muttered the fat boy in disgust, throwing himself down on the ground with rifle across his knees. "Lions! I don't believe there are any lions in the whole country. Dad's been having dreams. It's my private opinion that Dad's got an imagination that works over time once in a while. I think --- "

The words died on the fat boy's lips. His eyes grew wide, the pupils narrowed, the whites giving the appearance of small inverted saucers.

Stacy scarcely breathed.

There, slinking across an open space on the rise, its tail swishing its ears laid flat on its cruel, cat-like head, was a tawny, lithe creature.

Stacy Brown recognized the object at once. It was a mountain lion, a large one. It seemed to Chunky that he never had seen a beast as large in all his life. The lion was alternately listening to the baying of the hounds and peering about for a suitable tree in which to hide itself.

Stacy acted like a man in a trance. Without any clear

idea as to what he was doing, he rose slowly to his feet. At that instant the lion discovered him. It crouched down, its eyes like sparks of fire, scintillating and snapping.

All at once Stacy threw his gun to his shoulder and pulled the trigger. At least he thought he did. But no report came.

A yellow flash, a swish and the beast had leaped clear of the rise and disappeared even more suddenly than he had come.

"Wha -- wha --- " gasped Chunky. Then he made a discovery.

Chunky was holding the rifle by the barrel with the muzzle against his shoulder, having aimed the butt at the crouching lion. Chunky had had a severe attack of "buck fever."

With a wild yell that woke the echoes and sent Jim Nance and Professor Zepplin tearing through the bushes, Stacy dashed down the steep slope, forgetting to take his rifle with him in his hurried descent.

He met the two men running toward him.

"What is it? What's happened?" shouted the Professor.

"I saw him! I saw him!" yelled Stacy, almost frantic with excitement.

Nance grabbed the boy by the shoulder, shaking him roughly.

"Speak up. What did you see?"

"I su -- su -- saw a lu -- lu -- lion, I di -- did."

"Where?" demanded Nance.

"Up there."

Chunky's eyes were full of excitement.

"Why didn't you shoot him?"

"I -- I tried to, but the gu -- gun wouldn't go off. I -- I had it wrong end to."

Dad relaxed his grip on the fat boy's arm and sat down heavily.

"Of all the tarnal idiots -- of all! Professor, if we don't tie that boy to a tree he'll be killing us all with his fool ways. Why, you baby, you ain't fit to carry a pop-gun. By the way, where is your gun?"

"I -- I guess, I lost it up -- up there," stammered Stacy.

Dad started for the top of the rise in long strides, Chunky gazing after him in a dazed sort of way.

"I -- I guess I did make a fool of myself, didn't I, Professor?" he mourned.

"I am inclined to think you did -- several different varieties of them," answered Professor Zepplin in a tone of disgust.

CHAPTER XV

THE MYSTERY OF THE RIFLE

"I can't help it, I saw a lion, anyway," muttered the fat boy.

"Come up here!" It was Dad's voice calling to them. "Where's that rifle?"

"I -- I dropped it, I told you."

"Where did you drop it?"

"Right there."

"Show me."

Stacy climbed to the top of the rise and stepped confidently over to where he had let go the rifle before rushing down after having tried to shoot the lion. He actually stooped over to pick up the gun, so confident was he as to its location. Then a puzzled expression appeared on Stacy's face.

"Oh, it's there, is it?"

"Why -- I -- I ----- Say, you're trying to play a joke on me."

"I rather think you've played it on yourself," jeered the guide. "Where did you leave it?"

"Right there, I tell you."

"Sure you didn't throw it over in the bushes down the other side?"

"I guess I know what I did with it," retorted Chunky indignantly.

"Well, it isn't here." Dad was somewhat puzzled by this time. He saw that Stacy was very confident of having left the gun at that particular place, but it could not be found.

"Maybe somebody's stolen it," suggested the boy.

"Nonsense! Who is there here to steal it, in the first place? In the second, how could any one slip in here at the right moment and get away with your rifle?"

"You have no -- no idea what has become of it -- no theory?" asked the Professor.

"Not the least little bit," replied the guide.

"Most remarkable -- most remarkable," muttered Professor Zepplin. "I cannot understand it."

"We'll look around a bit," announced Dad.

The three men searched everywhere, even going all the way down to the base of the rise on either side, but nowhere did they find the slightest trace of the missing rifle. After they had returned to the summit, Dad, a new idea in mind, went over the rocks and the ground again in search of footprints. The only footprints observable were those of their own party. There was more in the mystery than Dad could fathom.

"Well, this gets me," declared the guide, wiping the perspiration from his forehead. "This certainly does."

"Is -- is my rifle lost?" wailed Chunky.

"I reckon you'll never see that pretty bit of firearms again," grinned Jim.

"But it must be here," insisted Stacy.

"But it isn't. Fortunately we have plenty of guns with us. You can get another when we go back to camp."

"Yes, but this one is mine --- "

"Was yours," corrected Nance.

"It is mine, and I'm going to have it before I leave this miserable old hole," declared the boy.

"I hope you find it. I'd like to know how the thing ever got away in that mysterious manner."

"Maybe the lion took it."

"Mebby he did. Funny I hadn't thought of that," answered Nance gravely. Then both he and the Professor burst into a shout of laughter.

They made their way slowly back to the point where they were to meet the others of the party. Chunky, now being without a rifle, was well content to remain with the guide and the Professor.

While all this was going on Tad and Walter were picking their way over the rough ridges, through narrow canyons, riding their ponies where a novice would hardly have dared to walk. The ponies seemed to take to the work naturally. Not a single misstep was made by either of them. They, too, could hear the dogs, but the latter were far away most of the time, even though, for all the riders knew, they might have been just the other side of the rocky wall along which the two boys were traveling.

They kept on in this way until late in the afternoon, when they stopped and dismounted, deciding that they would have a bite to eat.

"It doesn't look as if we were going to have any luck, does it, Tad?" asked Walter in a disappointed tone.

"No, it doesn't. But one never can tell. In hunting game you know it comes upon one suddenly. You have to be ever on the alert. We know that the dogs have been on the trail of something."

"Perhaps deer," suggested Walter.

"Yes, it is possible, though I don't know whether those dogs will trail deer or not. You know they may be trained to hunt lions. I didn't hear Mr.Nance say."

They were munching biscuit and eating oranges as they rested, which must have tasted good to them. The temperature was going down with the day, though the light was strong in the canyon where they were standing. Above them the jagged, broken cliffs rose tier on tier until they seemed to disappear far up in the fleecy clouds that were drifting lazily over the Canyon.

All at once Silver Face, Tad's pony, exhibited signs of restlessness, which seemed to be quickly communicated to the other animal. The pintos stamped, shook their heads and snorted.

"Whoa! What's wrong with you fellows?" demanded Tad, eyeing the ponies keenly. "Smell something, eh?"

"Maybe they smell oats," suggested Walter.

"I guess not. They are a long way from oats at the present moment."

Tad paused abruptly. A pebble had rattled down the rocky wall and bounded off some yards to the front of them. Silver Face started and would have bounded away had not a firm hand been at that instant laid on the bridle rein.

To one unaccustomed to the mountains the incident might have passed unnoticed. By this time Tad Butler was a pretty keen woodsman as well as plainsman. He had learned to take notice of everything. Even the most trivial signs hold a meaning all their own for the man who habitually lives close to Nature.

The lad glanced sharply at the rocks.

"See anything?" asked Walter.

"No."

"What did you think you heard?"

"I didn't hear anything but that pebble. The horses smelled something, though."

While he was speaking the lad's glances were traveling slowly over the rocks above. All at once he paused.

"Don't stir, Walt. Look up."

"Where?"

"In line with that cloud that looks like a dragon. Then lower your glance slowly. I think you will see something worth while."

It was a full moment before Walter Perkins discovered that to which his attention had been called.

"It's a cat," breathed Walt, almost in awe.

"Yes, that's a lion. He is evidently hiding up there, where he has gone to get away from the dogs. We will walk away a bit as if we were leaving. Then we'll tether the horses securely. Don't act as if you saw the beast. I know now what was the matter with the mustangs. They scented that beast up there."

The ponies were quickly secured, after which the boys crouched in the brush and sought out the lion again. He was still in the same place, but was now standing erect, head toward them, well raised as if in a listening attitude.

"My, isn't he a fine one!" whispered Walt. Walter Perkins was not suffering from the same complaint that

Chunky had caught when he first saw his lion over in the other canyon, an offshoot from the Bright Angel Canyon, and where he had lost his rifle so mysteriously.

"Take careful aim; then, when he turns his side toward us, let him have it," directed Tad.

"Oh, no, you discovered him. He is your game. You shoot, Tad."

Butler shook his head.

"I want you to shoot. I have already killed a cougar. This is your chance to distinguish yourself."

Walter's eyes sparkled. He raised his rifle, leveling it through the crotch of a small tree.

"Wait till he turns," whispered Tad, fingering his own rifle anxiously. He could hardly resist the temptation to take a shot at the animal where it stood facing them far up the side of the canyon wall.

"Now!" Tad's tone was calm, steady and low.

Walter's rifle barked.

"You've hit him!" yelled Tad. "Look out! He's up again!" warned the boy.

The beast had not been killed by the shot. He had been bowled over, dropping down to a lower crag, where he sprang to his feet and with a roar of rage bounded up the mountainside.

"Shoot! Shoot!" cried Butler.

But Walter did not even raise his rifle. A sudden fit of trembling had taken possession of him. His was the "buck fever" in another form.

Bang!

Butler had let go a quick shot.

A roar followed the shot.

"Bang!"

"There, I guess that settled him," decided Tad Butler, lowering his rifle.

"I -- I should say it did," gasped Walter.

The tawny beast was throwing himself this way and that, the boys meanwhile watching him anxiously.

"I'm afraid he's going to stick up there," cried Walter, dancing about shouting excitedly.

"No, he isn't. There he comes."

"Hurray!"

"Duck!"

Tad grabbed his companion, jerking the latter back and running with him. They were just at the spot where the ponies had been tethered, when a heavy body struck the ground not far from where they had been standing.

Silver Face leaped right up into the air, then settled back on his haunches in an attempt to break the hitching rope.

Tad struck the animal against the flank with the flat of his hand, whereat the mustang bounded to his feet.

"Whoa, you silly old animal!" cried Tad. "Look out, Walt, don't get too near that lion. You may lose some of your clothes if he shouldn't happen to be dead. I'll be there in a moment, as soon as I can get these horses quieted down."

In a moment Tad was running toward his companion.

"Is he settled?"

"I don't know. His -- his eyes are open," stammered Walter, standing off a safe distance from the prostrate beast.

Tad poked the animal with the muzzle of his rifle.

"Yes, he's a dead one. One less brute to make war on the deer. Won't old Dad be surprised when we trail into camp with this big game?" exulted the Pony Rider boy.

"Yes, but -- but how are we going to get the fellow there?" wondered Walter.

"Get him there? Well, I guess we'll do it somehow. I'll tell you what, I'll take him over the saddle in front of me. That's the idea. You bring out Silver Face and we'll see how he feels about it. I wouldn't be surprised if he raised a row."

Silver Face did object most emphatically. The instant the pony came in sight of the dead lion he sat down on his haunches. Tad urged and threatened, but not another inch would the pinto budge.

"I guess I know how to fix you," gritted the boy.

He was on the back of the sitting mustang, his feet in the stirrups, before the pony realized what had happened. A reasonably sharp rowel, pressed into the pinto's side, brought him a good two feet clear of the ground.

Then began a lively battle between the boy and the horse.

"Don't let him tread on the beast," shouted Walter.

"N-n-no danger of that," stammered Tad. It was a lively battle while it lasted, but Silver Face realized, as he had never done before, that he had met his master. After some twenty minutes of fight, in which the pinto made numerous futile attempts to climb the sheer side of the canyon at the imminent danger of toppling over backwards and crushing his master, the brute gave up.

"Now you hold him while I load on the beast," directed Tad, riding up.

This called for more disturbance. Silver Face fought against taking a lion on his back. He drew the line at that. Just the same, after another lively scrimmage, Mr.Lion was loaded on, but no sooner had Tad swung into the saddle than he swung out again. He hadn't even time to get his toes in the stirrups before he was flying through the air, head first. Walter had difficulty in determining which was boy and which was lion. The lion struck the ground first, Tad landing on top of him.

With rare presence of mind, Walter had seized the pinto and was having a lively set-to with the beast, with the odds in favor of Silver Face, when Tad sprang up and ran to his companion's assistance.

Tad's temper was up. The way he grilled Silver Face that animal perhaps never forgot. Not that Tad abused his mount. He never would be guilty of abusing a horse. He was too fond of horseflesh to do such a thing, but he knew how to punish an animal in other and more effective ways. Silver Face was punished.

"Now, my fine fellow, let's see who's boss here!" laughed Tad. "Hold him while I put aboard the baggage, Walt."

The pony submitted to the ordeal a second time. This time there was no bucking, and shortly afterwards the lads started for their companions bearing the trophy of their hunt with them.

CHAPTER XVI

A NEW WAY TO HUNT LIONS

Long before they reached the meeting point they heard the long-drawn "Woohoo!" of Jim Nance calling them in. They were the only ones out at that time. Tad set up a series of answering "woos-hoos" that caused Silver Face to wiggle his ears disapprovingly, as if this were some new method of torture invented for his special benefit.

As they got in sight of the rest of the party, the boys set up a shout. Their companions, about that time, discovered that Tad was carrying something before him on the pony. Chunky and Ned started on a run to meet Tad and Walter. How Chunky did yell when he discovered what that something was.

"They've got a cat! They've got a cat!" he howled, dancing about and swinging his arms. "I tell you, they've got a cat!"

Tad rode into camp smiling, flinging the lion to the ground, which caused Tad's pony to perform once more.

"Who shot him?" cried the Professor, fully as excited as the boys.

"This is a partnership cat," laughed Tad. "We both have some bullets in him. How many did you fellows get?"

"Well, I had one, but he got away," answered Stacy, his face sobering instantly. "And -- and he carried off my rifle too."

"What's that?" demanded Tad.

Chunky explained briefly. But he had little opportunity to talk. Dad, who had been examining the dead lion, straightened up and looked at Tad.

"Good job, boys. It's a dandy. Must weigh nigh onto three hundred pounds. Have much of a tussle with him?"

"Not any. He was dead when he got down to us."

"Very fine specimen," decided the Professor, examining the dead beast from a respectable distance. "You lads are to be congratulated."

"Say, I'm going with you to-morrow," cried Stacy. "These folks don't know how to hunt lions."

"Do you?" demanded Nance witheringly.

Stacy colored violently.

"At least I know how to stalk them," he answered. "If I lose my gun in the excitement that doesn't mean that I'm not a natural born lion chaser. Anybody can shoot a lion, but everybody can't sit still and charm the lion right up to him."

They admitted that the fat boy was right in this assertion. Chunky had done all of that. Upon their return to camp, Walter and Tad had asked numerous questions about the loss of the gun. There was little additional information that either Stacy or the two men could give them. The gun had most mysteriously disappeared, that was all. Nance was more puzzled than any of the others and he groped in vain for an explanation of the mystery, but no satisfactory explanation suggested itself to his mind.

After supper the guide cut some meat from the cat and fed it to the weary dogs, who had not succeeded in treeing a single lion, though they had come near doing so several times. But they had sent the cats flying for cover, which had given Chunky and the other two boys opportunity to use their guns, though Stacy Brown, in his excitement, had failed to take advantage of the opportunity offered to him.

It was decided that the hunt should be taken up again on the following morning. Nance said Stacy might go with Tad this time, Nance taking charge of the other three boys. This was satisfactory to Chunky and Tad.

The morning found the camp awake at an early hour. Chunky and Tad set off together, the former having been equipped with a rifle from the extra supply carried by the party, the guide having administered a sarcastic suggestion that Chunky tie the rifle to his back so that he would not lose this one.

Chunky made appropriate reply, after which they rode away. The early part of the day was devoid of success. They did not even hear the bay of a hound all the forenoon. Tad took their quest coolly, undisturbed. He had already gotten one lion and could well afford not to get one this time. It was different with Stacy. He was anxious to distinguish himself, to make amends for his blunders of the previous day.

About an hour after they had eaten their lunch they heard the bounds for the first time. Tad listened intently for a few minutes.

"I think they are coming this way, Chunky."

"If they do, you give me the first shot. I've simply got to meet another cat."

"You shall have it, providing you are on the job and ready. These cats don't wait around for a fellow to get ready to shoot, as you have no doubt observed."

"Don't remind me of disagreeable things, please," growled Stacy. "I've had my chance and I lost it. Next time I see a cat I'm going to kill him on the spot. Wait; I'm going to take an observation."

"Don't go far," warned Tad.

"No, I won't. Just want to have a look at the landscape," flung back Stacy, hurrying away, while Tad stretched out for a little rest, well satisfied to have Stacy do the moving about until there was something real to be done, when Tad would be on hand on the jump.

Stacy had not taken his gun. In fact, he wholly forgot to do so, not thinking for an instant that he would have opportunity to use it. This was where the fat boy made another serious mistake. A hunter should never be beyond reaching distance of his gun when out on the trail for game. It is a mistake that has cost some men their lives, others the loss of much coveted game.

Choosing a low, bushy pinyon tree as best suited to the purposes of a lazy climber, Stacy climbed it, grunting and grumbling unintelligibly. He had hopes that he might discover something worth while, something that would distinguish him from his fellows on that particular day.

"I feel as if something were going to happen," he confided to the tree, seating himself in a crotch formed by a limb extending out from the main body of the tree, then parting the foliage for a better view. "It's funny how a fellow feels about these things some times. Hello, there, I actually believe those are deer running yonder. Or maybe they're cows," added Stacy. "Anyhow I couldn't shoot them, whichever they are, so I won't get excited over them."

Chunky fixed his eyes on the opposite side of the tree a little above where he was perched.

"I thought I saw something move there. Hello, I hear the hounds again. They've surely gotten on track of something. And --- "

Once more the fat boy paused. He saw something yellow lying along a limb of the tree, something at first sight that he took to be a snake. But he knew of no snakes that had fur on their bodies. The round, furry thing that he thought might be a snake at first now began whipping up and down on the limb, curling at its end, twisting, performing strange antics.

What could it mean? Stacy parted the foliage a little more, then once again, as had been the case on the previous day, his eyes opened wide.

He saw now what was at the other end of the snake-like appendage. And seeing he understood that he was in a predicament. But Chunky's voice failed him.

There on the opposite limb of the tree, less than ten feet away, crouched the biggest mountain lion Stacy Brown ever had seen. And it grew larger with the seconds. The beast was working its tail, its whiskers bristled, its eyes shone like points of steel. It seemed as if the beast were trying to decide whether to attack the boy within such easy reach or to leap to the ground and flee. The deep baying of the dogs in the distance evidently decided the cat against the latter plan. Then, too, perhaps the howls that Chunky now emitted had something to do with the former question.

Tad Butler, stretched out on the ground, found himself standing bolt upright as if he had been propelled to that position by a spring. The most unearthly howls he had ever heard broke upon the mountain stillness.

"Wow! Ow-wow-wow! Tad! Help, help, help! Quick!"

Tad was off like a shot himself, not even pausing to snatch up his gun which lay so near at hand. And how he did run!

"Where, Chunky? Where are you? Shout quick!"

"Wow! Ow-wow-wow!" was the only answer Stacy Brown could make, but the sound of his voice unerringly guided Tad to the location. But Stacy could not be found.

"In the name of --- "

"Wow! Ow-wow-wow!" howled the agonized voice of the fat boy from the branches of the pinyon tree.

Tad peered up between the branches. He saw Stacy looking down upon him with panic stricken gaze.

"For the love of goodness, what's the matter, Stacy? You nearly frightened me to death."

"Look out!" The words, shouted at the top of the fat boy's voice, were so thrilling that Tad leaped back instinctively.

"See here, don't make a fool of me, too. What's the matter with you? Come down out of that."

"I can't. He'll get me."

"What will get you? Nothing will get you, you ninny!"

"The lion will get me."

"Have you gone raving mad on the subject of lions?" jeered Butler.

"Look, if you don't believe me. He's up here. He's trying to get a bite out of me. Shoot him, as you love me, Tad; shoot and shoot straight or I'm a dead one."

For the first time since his arrival on the scene Tad began to realize that Stacy was not having fun with him. Something really was up that tree -- something besides a Pony Rider boy.

"You don't mean to tell me there's a cat up there --- "

"Yes, yes! He's over there on the other side. Shoot, shoot!"

"I haven't my gun with me."

The fat boy groaned helplessly.

"I'm a dead one! Nothing can save me. Tell them I died like a man; tell them I never uttered a squeal."

Tad had sprung around to the side of the pinyon tree indicated by Chunky. Up there on a bushy limb, clear of the heavier foliage, lay a sleek, but ugly looking cat, swishing its tail angrily. First, its glances would shoot over to Stacy Brown, then down to Tad Butler. The lion, as Tad decided on the spot, had gone into the tree to hide from the dogs as had the one that had been shot on the canyon wall the previous afternoon. This time the proposition was a different one. Both boys were in dire peril, as Tad well knew. At any second the cat might spring, either at him or at Stacy. And neither boy had a gun in his hands.

Tad's mind worked with lightning-like rapidity. It was a time for quick thinking if one expected to save one's skin from being torn by those needle-like claws. Butler thought of a plan. He did not know whether there were one chance in a million of the plan working. He wanted that lion a great deal more than the lion wanted him. He was going to take a desperate chance. An older and more experienced man might not have cared to try what Tad Butler was about to attempt.

The Pony Rider boy's hand slipped down to the lasso hanging from his belt. He was thankful that he had that. The lasso was always there except when he was in the saddle, when it was usually looped over the pommel.

"Chunky, yell! Make all the noise you can."

"I am. Wow-ow-wow. Y-e-o-w wow!"

"That's right, keep it up. Don't stop. Make faces at him, make believe you're going to jump at --- "

"Say, anybody would think this were a game of croquet and that I was trying to make the other fellow miss the wicket. Don't you think --- "

"I'm trying to get you to attract his attention --- "

"I don't want to attract his attention. I want the beast to look the other way," wailed the fat boy. "I want to get out of here."

"Well, why haven't you?"

"I dassent."

While carrying on this conversation with his chum, Tad was watching the cat narrowly. The animal was showing signs of greater excitement now. The boy decided that the beast was preparing to jump one way or another -- which way was a matter of some concern to both boys at that particular instant.

The cat took two long paces in Stacy's direction. Stacy emitted the most blood-curdling yell Tad had ever heard. It served Butler's very purpose. The beast halted with one hind foot poised in the air, glaring at Stacy, who was howling more lustily than ever.

Swish!

Tad's lariat shot through the air. His aim was true, his hand steady and cool.

CHAPTER XVII

THE WHIRLWIND BALL OF YELLOW

When the startled cat felt the touch of the raw-hide rope against its leg it made a tremendous leap straight ahead.

"Too late!" clicked Tad. "That loop is taut on you now!"

"M-m-murder! Look out!" bellowed Stacy.

For the cat's leap had carried it straight at the fat boy. In fact one sharp set of claws raked the lad from shoulder to waist, though without more than breaking the skin.

That blow settled Stacy.

"I'm dead -- ripped to pieces!" he yelled.

Without waiting to jump from the tree, Stacy simply fell. Over and over on the ground he rolled until he was a dozen yards away from the tree.

"If you're dead," Tad grinned, "get up and come over here, and tell me about it."

Stacy slowly rose to his feet. He was badly shaken, covered with dirt and with some blood showing through the rents in his clothes.

"Nothing but my presence of mind and my speed saved me, anyway," Chunky grumbled ruefully.

All in a twinkling that whirling yellow ball shot out of the tree, striking the ground before Tad Butler could draw the rope taut. However, the rope still hung over a limb. How the dirt flew! Tad realized that swift action must come ere the beast should make a leap at them.

Stacy started away, but Butler's sharp tone halted him.

"Chunky!" Tad panted.

"What?"

"Get hold of this rope with me. Shake yourself. What ails you? Have you got a streak of yellow in you?"

"I can thrash the fellow who says I have?" roared the fat boy, springing to his feet.

"That's the way to talk. Come, hurry -- get hold here! He's too much for me and he's going to get away from me if you don't lend a hand."

"Wh-what do you want me to do?"

"Grab hold of this rope, I tell you."

Chunky did so, but keeping a wary eye on the rolling, tumbling, spitting yellow ball, which was a full grown mountain lion, and an ugly brute. The king of the canyons, however, was in a most humiliating position for a king of any sort. He had been roped by his left hind foot, the other end of the rope being in the hands of the intrepid Pony Rider boy, Thaddeus Butler. Tad knew well that he had a good thing and he proposed to hang on as long as there was an ounce of strength left in his body. By this time Stacy had gotten a grip on the rope.

"Now pull steadily until I tell you to stop."

Slowly, digging his claws into the dirt, biting at the rope that held him fast, the cat was drawn toward the pinyon tree despite all his struggles. Tad's object was to pull the beast off its feet, in which position it would be unable to do very much damage.

Perhaps the cat realized something of this, for all of a sudden it sprang to the base of the tree and with a roar landed up among the lower limbs.

Ere the beast even felt the touch of the tree limb under its feet, the brave Chunky was several rods away peering from behind a rock, howling like a Comanche Indian.

Tad, too, had made some lively moves. The instant he saw that the cat was going to jump he took a quick twist about the tree, shortening the rope until it was taut. He made a quick knot, then leaped back out of the way. But none too soon. The cat pounced on the spot where he had been standing, narrowly missing the boy. But the rope was free of the limb of the tree over which it had been first drawn. The beast was free to gambol about as far as the rope would permit.

The boy's mind was still working rapidly.

"Run to the guns, Chunky. Shoot and keep shooting until you attract the attention of the rest of the party. We've got to have help. We never shall be able to handle him ourselves, and I want to save him."

Stacy hesitated.

"Run, I tell you!" shouted Butler. "Don't stand there like a statue. Go!"

Chunky jumped as if he had been hit, and ran limping toward the place where they had left their weapons and their mustangs. He found both, though Chunky was too excited to notice the ponies at all. Already they were restless, having scented the mountain lion.

Snatching up his own rifle, Stacy fired six shots in rapid succession. Then grabbing the other gun, he let six more go, but continued snapping the firing pin on the empty chamber after all the cartridges had been exploded, before he realized that he was not shooting at all. Stacy in trying to reload fumbled and made a mess of it, spilling a lot of shells on the ground, most of which he was unable to find again.

"We got him! We got him!" the fat boy kept chuckling to himself. "We certainly have done it this time."

Finally he got one gun loaded, and had fired it off six times when he heard Tad Butler's "Whoo-e-e-e-e."

Chunky hurried back to his companion.

"They've answered," called Tad.

In the meantime the latter had been having a lively time. He knew that were he to give the least possible chance the beast would bite the rope off and escape even if he did no worse. It was to prevent this that the boy exerted all his ingenuity and effort. This consisted of whoops and howls, throwing rocks at the animal, dodging in now and then to whack the lion with a piece from a limb that had been broken down by the cat in its thrashing above.

The dust was flying. At times it seemed as if the lion must have gotten the hardy Pony Rider boy. At such times the lithe, active form of Tad Butler could be seen leaping from the cloud of dust while the beast followed with savage lunges to the end of its rope. It seemed impossible to tire out either boy or cat.

It was this condition of affairs that Stacy Brown came upon on his return. He stood gazing at the scene, fascinated.

"Look out, Tad! He'll get you!" shouted the boy.

"Get in here and give him a poke in the ribs," cried Butler.

"Not for a million dollars, badly as I need money," returned the fat boy. "What do you take me for, an animal trainer?"

"Then I'll have to keep on doing it till Mr.Nance gets here to help me. This is the greatest thing we've ever done, old boy!"

"Yes, it'll be a great thing when the brute hands you one from those garden rakes of his. Get away and I'll shoot him," directed Stacy, swinging his rifle into position.

"Put that gun down!" thundered Tad. "You'll be winging me next thing you do. Put it down, I say!"

Stacy grumblingly obeyed. Meanwhile the gymnastic exercise continued with unabated vigor. There was not an instant's pause. The mountain lion was busier perhaps than it ever had been in its life. It was battling for its life, too, and it knew it.

Once Tad was raked from head to foot by a vicious claw, but the Pony Rider boy merely laughed. His endurance, too, was most remark able. Stacy would hardly get within gun-shot of the beast, always standing near a tree convenient for climbing. Tad was not saying much now. He was rather too busy for conversation. At last the report of a rifle was heard not far away.

"Answer them. It's the gang," called Tad. Chunky fired a shot into the air, following it with four others. It was only a short time before Jim Nance with Professor Zepplin and the two other boys came dashing up, shouting to know where Tad and Chunky were. They saw Chunky first, on guard with his rifle as if holding off an enemy.

"What's the trouble?" cried Nance.

"We've got him! We've got him!" yelled Stacy.

About that time Nance discovered the swirling cloud of dust, from which at intervals emerged a yellow ball. The guide caught the significance of the scene at a single glance.

"It's a cat," howled Ned. "Let me shoot him."

"Put away your guns. I guess we know how to catch lions in a scientific manner," declared Stacy.

"They've roped the cat," snapped the guide. "Beats anything I ever heard of." He was off his mustang instantly and running toward Tad. "Keep him busy, keep him busy, boy. I'll fix him for you in a minute."

"I don't want you to kill him."

"I'm not going to. We've got to stretch him."

Tad did not know what stretching meant in this particular instance, but he was soon to learn. Nance got off to one side of the busy scene, then directed Tad to ease up a bit. The boy did so. He saw that Dad, too, was planning to use his lariat, though the boy had no idea in what way. The cat instantly sat down and began tearing at its bonds. All at once Nance's rope shot through the air. It caught the lion fairly around the neck.

For a few moments the air was full of streaks of yellow. The cat was now fast at both ends. The neck hold was the worse of the two, for it choked the beast and soon tired him out.

"Now stretch him," directed the guide.

"How do you mean?"

"Take a single hitch about the tree with your rope, so

that we can straighten him out."

This Tad did, while Nance performed a similar service on his own line, being careful not to choke the lion to death. During this latter part of the proceeding the party that had up to that time held off, now approached.

"Will he bite?" asked Walter.

"Stick your finger in his mouth and see?" jeered Chunky. "He can scratch, too. But we got him, didn't we? We're the original lion tamers from the wild and woolly West."

"Come, who is going to tie those claws together, Stacy?" demanded the guide.

"Do what?"

"Tie the cat's feet together."

"Let the Professor do it. He hasn't done anything yet on this trip. Besides, I've got to stand here ready to shoot if the lion gets away. If it weren't for that I'd tie his feet."

"Here, you tie his feet, then. I'll handle the gun," volunteered Ned, stepping forward.

Chunky drew back.

"If some one will hold my end of the line I'll attend to that little matter," said Tad.

"I guess it's time I did something around here,"

interjected Ned. "What do you want me to do, Mr.Nance?"

"Take your rope, watch your opportunity and rope the forward legs. After that is done have somebody hold the rope while you tie the feet securely together."

Ned roped the feet without further question, then handing the line to Walter Perkins, he calmly tied together the feet of the snarling, spitting beast. The same was done with the hind feet, though the latter proved to be much more dangerous than the forward feet. But the mouth of the animal was still free. He could bite and he did make desperate efforts to get at his captors. They took good care that he did not reach them. Chunky suggested that they pull the cat's teeth, so he couldn't bite. Tad wanted to know if they couldn't put a muzzle on.

"The question is what are you going to do with him, now that you have him?" demanded the Professor.

"That's the first sane word that's been spoken since we arrived here," grinned Nance.

"We are going to take him back to camp, of course," declared Tad.

"Of course we are. Don't you understand, we're going to take him back to camp," affirmed Stacy.

"What's your plan, Butler?" asked Nance.

"If you leave it to me, I'll show you."

"Go ahead."

Tad cut a long, tough sapling. This, after some effort, he managed to pass through the loop made by the bound legs of the lion. This strung the beast on the pole.

"Now, we'll fasten the two ends to two ponies," decided the lad.

Silver Face and Walter's pony having been broken in on the previous day, these two were chosen to carry the prize. They did not object, and in a short time the procession started off for camp, with the lion, back down, strung on the pole between two ponies, snarling, spitting, roaring out his resentment, while Chunky, leading the way, was singing at the top of his voice:

"Tad Butler is the man; he goes to all the shows, he sticks his head in the lion's mouth and tells you all he knows.Who-o-o-pe-e-e!"

CHAPTER XVIII

THE UNWILLING GUEST DEPARTS

Jim Nance didn't say much, but from the way he looked at Tad Butler, a quizzical smile playing about the corners of his mouth, it was plain that he was filled with admiration for the young Pony Rider who could take a lion practically single-handed.

As yet the story of the capture had not been told. Their prize must first be taken care of. This part of the affair Nance looked after personally. He found a few strands of wire in his kit and with these he made a collar and a wire leader that led out to where the tough lariat began. To this the lion was fastened, his forefeet left bound, the hind feet being liberated In this condition he was tied to a tree in the camp in Bright Angel Gulch.

Chunky was not sure that he liked the arrangement. He was wondering whether lions were gifted with the proverbial memory of elephants. If so, and if the big cat should get loose in the night, Chunky knew what would happen to himself. The boy determined to sleep with one eye open, his rifle beside his bed. He would die fighting bravely for his life. He was determined upon that.

Around the camp fire a jolly party of boys gathered

that night after supper, their merry conversation interrupted occasionally by a snarling and growling from the captive.

"Now, young gentlemen, we are anxious to hear the story of the capture," said the Professor.

"Oh, it was nothing," answered Stacy airily. "It was nothing for us. Shooting cats is too tame for such hunters as Tad and me. We just saw him up a tree -- that is, I saw him, and --- "

"Where were you?" interrupted Nance.

"I was up the same tree," answered Stacy.

"I'll bet the cat treed him," shouted Ned Rector. "How about it, Tad?"

"Chunky's telling the story. Let him tell it in his own way."

"I'll tell you about it, fellows. I was up a tree looking for lions. I found one. He was sitting in the same tree with me. He was licking his chops. You see, he wanted a slice of me, I'm so tender and so delicious --- "

"So is a rhinoceros," interjected Ned.

"If the gentleman will wait until I have finished he may have the floor to himself. Well, that's about all. I yelled for Tad. He came running, and he roped the cat."

"Then what did you do?" questioned Walter.

"Oh, I fell out of the tree. Look at this!" shouted Stacy

as soon as he was able to make himself heard above the laughter, pointing to his ripped clothes. "That's where the beast made a pass at me. I'm wounded, I am; wounded in a hand-to-hand conflict with the king of the canyon. How would that read in the Chillicothe 'Gazette' I'm going to dash off something after this fashion to send them: 'Stacy Brown, our distinguished fellow citizen, globe-trotter, hunter of big game and nature lover, was seriously wounded last week in the Grand Canyon of Arizona --- '"

"In what part of your anatomy is the Grand Canyon located?" questioned Ned Rector. "I rise for information."

"The Grand Canyon is where the Pony Rider Boys store their food," returned Stacy quickly. "Where did I leave off?"

"You were lost in the Canyon," reminded Walter.

"Oh, yes. 'Was seriously wounded in the Grand Canyon in a desperate battle with the largest lion ever caught in the mountains. Assisted by Thaddeus Butler, also of Chillicothe, Mr.Brown succeeded in capturing the lion alive, after his bloodstained garments had been nearly stripped from his person.'"

"The lion's bloodstained garments?" inquired Walter mildly.

"No, mine, of course. 'Mr. Brown, it is said, will recover from his wounds, though he will bear the scars of the conflict the rest of his life.' Ahem! I guess that will hold the boys on our block for a time," finished Chunky, swelling out his chest. "Yes, that'll make them prisoners for life," agreed Ned Rector.

"I think I shall have to edit that account before it goes to the paper," declared Professor Zepplin.

"How can you edit it when you didn't see the affair?" demanded Chunky.

"Editors are not supposed to see beyond the point of the pencil they are using," answered Ned. "But they know the failings of the fellows who do the writing."

"What do you know about it? You never were an editor," scoffed Stacy.

"No, but I'd like to be for about an hour after your article reached the 'Gazette' office."

"How about giving that cat something to eat, Mr.Nance?" asked Tad, thus changing the subject.

The guide shook his head.

"He wouldn't eat; at least not for a while."

"What do lions eat?" asked Walter.

"That one tried to eat me," replied Stacy. "I don't like the look in his eye at all. It says, just as plain as if it were printed, 'I'd like to have you served up _a-la-mode_.'"

At this juncture, Jim Nance walked over; with a burning brand in hand, to look at the cat's fastenings. The lion jumped at him. Jim poked the firebrand into the animal's face, which sent the cat back the full length of his tether. After examining the fastenings carefully, Nance pronounced them so secure that the beast would not get away.

The ponies had been tethered some distance from where the prize was tied, the dogs being placed with the ponies so that they might not be disturbed by the captive during the night and thus keep the camp awake with their barks and growls.

After a time all hands went to bed, crawling into their blankets, where they were soon fast asleep. Late in the night Nance sat up. He thought he had heard the lion growl. Stepping to the door of the tent he listened. Not a sound could be heard save the mysterious whisperings of the Canyon. Jim went back to bed, not to awaken until the sun was up on the following morning.

Tad Butler, hearing the guide rise after daylight, turned out at the same time. Tad stepped outside, his first thought being for the captive. The Pony Rider boy's eyes grew large as he gazed at the tree where the cat had been left the evening before. There was no lion there.

"Hey, Mr.Nance, did you move the cat?"

"No. Why?"

"He isn't where we left him last night."

"What?" Nance was out on the jump. "Sure as you're alive he's gone. Now doesn't that beat all?"

Tad had hurried over to the place where he stood gloomily surveying the scene.

"I wonder where the rope and wire are?"

"That's so. He must have carried the whole business with him."

"How could he? How could he have untied the wire from the tree? There is something peculiar about this affair, Dad."

Whatever Dad's opinion might have been, he did not express it at the moment. Instead he got down on all fours, examining the ground carefully, going over every inch of it for several rods about the scene.

"Well this does git me," he declared, standing up, scratching his head reflectively.

By that time the rest of the party had come out.

"The lion's gone," shouted Tad.

"What, my lion got away?" wailed Chunky. "And he didn't take a chunk out of me to carry away with him?"

"I had no idea we could hold him. Of course he gnawed the rope in two," nodded the Professor.

"He didn't get loose of his own accord, sir," replied the guide.

"Then you don't mean to tell me that some person or persons liberated him?"

"I don't mean to tell you anything, because I don't know anything about it. I never was so befuddled in my life. I'm dead-beat, Professor."

Tad was gloomy. He had hoped to take the lion home with them, having already planned where he would keep the beast until the town, which he thought of presenting it to, had prepared a place for the gift. Now his hopes had been dashed. He had no idea that they would be able to get another lion. It was not so easy as all that. But how had the beast gotten away? There was a mystery about it fully as perplexing as had been the loss of Stacy's rifle. Tad was beginning to think, with Dad, that mysterious forces were, indeed, at work in the Grand Canyon.

While he was brooding over the problem, Chunky, emulating the movements of the guide, was down on hands and knees, examining the ground.

"Find any footprints?" called Ned in a jeering voice.

Stacy did not reply. His brow was wrinkled; his face wore a wise expression.

"Look out that you don't get bitten," warned Walter mischievously.

"By what?" demanded Stacy, glancing up.

"Footprints," answered Ned.

"Could any person have gotten in here and let the cat go without our having heard him, Mr.Nance?" asked Tad Butler.

"I reckon he couldn't."

"Did you hear anything in the night, Nance?" questioned the Professor.

"Come to think of it, I did get up once. I heard the cat growling, or thought I did, but after I had looked out and seen nothing, nor heard anything, I went back to bed again and didn't know anything more till sun-up. I guess I'm pretty slow. I'm getting old for a certainty."

"No; there is something peculiar, something very strange about this affair, Professor," spoke up Tad.

"Due wholly to natural causes," declared the Professor.

"No, I reckon you're wrong there, Professor," said Nance. "I'd have understood natural causes. It's the unnatural causes that gets a fellow."

"I've spotted it, I've spotted it! I know who freed the lion!" howled Stacy.

All hands rushed to him.

"Who, what, how, where, when?" demanded five voices at once.

"Yes, sir, I've found it. That lion --- "

"Don't joke," rebuked the Professor.

"I'm not joking. I know what I'm talking about. That cat was let go by a one-legged Indian. Now maybe you won't say I'm not a natural born sleuth," exclaimed the fat boy proudly.

CHAPTER XIX

THE FAT BOY DOES A GHOST DANCE

"A one-legged Indian?" chorused the lads.

"He's crazy," grumbled Dad. "He has cat on the brain."

"That's better than having nothing but hair on the brain," retorted Stacy witheringly.

"How do you know a one-legged Indian has been here?" questioned Tad, seeing that Chunky was in earnest.

"Look here," said the boy, pointing to a moccasin print in the soft turf at that point. "There's the right foot. Where's the left? Why there wasn't any left, of course. He had only one foot."

"Then he must have carried a crutch," laughed Ned. "Look for the crutch mark and then you'll have the mystery solved."

Jim Nance chuckled. Stacy regarded the guide with disapproving eyes.

"Tell me so I can laugh too," begged Chunky soberly.

"Why, you poor little tenderfoot, don't you know how that one track got there?"

Chunky shook his head.

"Well, that cowardly half breed that you call Chow was crossing the rocks here when the cat made a pass at him. Chow made a long leap. One foot struck there, the other about ten feet the other side. He hadn't time to put the second foot down else the cat would have got him. A one-legged Indian! Oh, help!"

"Haw-haw-haw!" mocked Stacy, striding away disgustedly while the shouts of his companions were ringing in his burning ears.

But the mystery was unsolved. Tad did not believe it ever would be, though he never ceased puzzling over it for a moment. That day no one got a lion, though on the second day following Ned Rector shot a small cat. Tad did not try to shoot. He wandered with Chunky all over the peaks and through the Canyon in that vicinity trying to rope more lions.

"You let that job out," ordered the guide finally. "Don't you know you're monkeying with fire? First thing you know you won't know anything. One of these times a cat'll put you to sleep for a year of Sundays."

"I guess you are right. Not that I am afraid, but there is no sense in taking such long chances. I'll drop it. I ought to be pretty well satisfied with what I have done."

Tad kept his word. He made no further attempts to rope mountain lions.

In the succeeding few days three more cats were shot. It was on the night of the fourth day after the escape of the captive that at something very exciting occurred in Camp Butler.

The camp was silent, all its occupants sound asleep, when suddenly they were brought bounding from their cots by frightful howls and yells of fear. The howls came from the tent of Stacy Brown. Stacy himself followed, leaping out into what they called the company street, dancing up and down, still howling at the top of his voice. Clad in pajamas, the fat boy was unconsciously giving a clever imitation of an Indian ghost dance.

Professor Zepplin was the first to reach the fat boy. He gave Chunky a violent shaking, while Nance was darting about the camp to see that all was right. He saw nothing unusual.

"What is the meaning of this, young man?" demanded the Professor.

"I seen it, I seen it," howled Stacy.

"What did you see?"

"A ghost! I seen a ghost!"

"You mean you 'saw' a ghost, not you 'seen'," corrected the Professor.

"I tell you I *seen* a ghost. I guess if you'd seen a ghost you wouldn't stop to choose words. You'd just howl like a lunatic in your own natural language --- "

Dad hastily threw more wood on the dying camp fire.

"I guess you had a nightmare," suggested Tad.

"It wasn't a mare, it was a man," persisted Stacy.

"He's crazy. Pity he doesn't catch sleeping sickness," scoffed Ned.

"Tell us what you did see," urged the Professor in a milder tone.

"I -- I was sleeping in -- in there when all at once I woke up --- "

"You thought you did, perhaps," nodded Walter.

"I didn't think anything of the sort. I know I did. Maybe I'd heard something. Well, I woke up and there -- and there --- " Chunky's eyes grew big, he stared wildly across the camp fire as if the terrifying scene were once more before him. "I woke up."

"You have told us that before," reminded Dad, who had joined the group.

"I woke up --- "

"That makes four times you woke up," laughed Ned. "You must, indeed, have had a restless night."

"I woke up --- "

"What again?"

"You wouldn't laugh if you'd seen what I saw" retorted

the fat boy, with serious face. "There, right at the entrance of the tent, was a ghost!"

"What kind of a ghost?" asked Dad.

"Just a ghost-ghost. It was all white and shiny and -- br-r-r-r!" shivered the boy. "It grinning. I could see right through it!"

"You must be an X-ray machine," declared Tad, chuckling.

"It didn't need anything of that sort. He was so shimmery that you could see right through him."

"What became of the spook? Did he fly up?" asked the guide.

"No, the spook just spooked," replied Stacy.

"How do you mean?" questioned Professor Zepplin.

"He thawed out like a snowball, just melted away when I yelled."

"Very thrilling, very thrilling. Most remarkable. A matter for scientific investigation," muttered the Professor, but whether he were in earnest or not the boys could not gather from his expressionless countenance.

"What did Chunky have for supper?" asked Walter.

"What didn't he have?" scoffed the guide. "We have to eat fast or we wouldn't get enough to keep up our strength."

"I guess I don't get any more than my share," retorted Stacy. "I have to work for that, too."

"Well, I'm going to bed," announced Ned Rector. "You fellows may sit up here and tell ghost stories all the rest of the night if you want to. It's me for the feathers."

"You're right, Ned," agreed Tad. "We are a lot of silly boys to be so upset over a fellow who has had a crazy nightmare. Professor, don't you think you ought to give Stacy some medicine?"

"Yes, give him something to make him sleep," chuckled Walter.

The boy was interrupted by a roar from Ned Rector's tent. Ned was shouting angrily. He burst out into the circle of light shed by the camp fire, waving his hands above his head.

"They've got mine, they've got mine!" he yelled, dancing about with a very good imitation of the ghost dance so recently executed by the fat boy.

"Got what?" demanded Dad sternly, striding forward.

"Somebody's stolen my rifle. The spook's robbed me. It's gone and all my cartridges and my revolver and ---"

The camp was in an uproar instantly. Chunky was nodding with satisfaction.

"It wasn't stolen. The spook just spooked it, that's all," he declared convincingly.

"But you must be in error, Ned," cried the Professor.

"I'm not. It's gone. I left it beside my bed. It isn't there now. I tell you somebody's been in this camp and robbed me!"

A sudden silence settled over the camp. The boys looked into each other's faces questioningly. Was this another mystery of the Bright Angel Gulch? They could not understand.

"Mebby the kid did see a ghost after all," muttered the guide.

"The kid did. And I guess the kid ought to know," returned Stacy pompously.

CHAPTER XX

IN THE HOME OF THE HAVASUPAIS

An investigation showed that Ned Rector was right in his assertion. His rifle had been taken, likewise his revolver and his cartridges. It lent color to Stacy's statement that he had seen something, but no one believed that that something had been a ghost, unless perhaps the guide believed it, for having lived close to Nature so long, he might be a superstitious person.

There was little sleep in the camp of the Pony Rider Boys for the rest of the night. They were too fully absorbed in discussing the events of the evening and the mysteries that seemed to surround them. First, Stacy had lost his rifle, the captive lion had mysteriously disappeared, and now another member of their party had lost his rifle and revolver. Dad directed the boys not to move about at all. He hoped to find a trail in the morning, a trail that would give him a clue in case prowlers had been in the camp.

A search in the morning failed to develop anything of the sort. Not the slightest trace of a stranger having visited the camp was discovered. They gave up -- the mystery was too much for them.

That day Nance decided to move on. Their camp was

to remain at the same place, but the half breed was directed to sleep by day and to stay on guard during the night. Jim proposed to take his charges into the wonderful Cataract Canyon, where they would pay a visit to the village of the Havasupai Indians.

This appealed to the Pony Riders. They had seen no Indians since coming to the Grand Canyon. They did not know that there were Indians ranging through that rugged territory, red men who were as familiar with the movements of the Pony Rider Boys as were the boys themselves.

They arrived at the Cataract Canyon on the morning of the second day, having visited another part of Bright Angel Gulch for a day en route.

At the entrance to the beautiful canyon the guide paused to tell them something about it.

"I will tell you," he said, "how the Havasupais came to select this canyon for their home. When the several bands of red men, who afterwards became the great tribes of the south-west, left their sacred Canyon -- mat-aw-we'-dit-ta -- by direction of their Moses -- Ka-that-ka-na'-ve -- to find new homes, the Havasupai family journeyed eastward on the trail taken by the Navajos and the Hopi. One night they camped in this canyon. Early the next day they took up their burdens to continue on their journey. But as they were starting a little papoose began to cry. The Kohot of the family, believing this to be a warning from the Great Spirit, decided to remain in the canyon.

"They found this fertile valley, containing about five hundred acres of level land. They called the place Hava-sua, meaning 'Blue Water,' and after a time they themselves were known, as Havasupai -- 'Dwellers By the Blue water'. They have been here ever since."

"Most interesting, most interesting," breathed the Professor. "But how comes it that this level stretch of fertile land is found in this rugged, rocky canyon, Nance?"

"That's easily answered. During hundreds of years the river has deposited vast quantities of marl at the upper ends of this valley. Thus four great dams have been built up forming barriers across the canyon. These dams have quite largely filled up, leaving level stretches of land of great richness."

"Do they work the land?" asked Tad.

"In a primitive way, they do, probably following the methods they learned from the cliff dwellers, who occupied the crude dwellings you have seen all along these walls in the canyons here."

The Cataract Canyon proved to be the most interesting of all that the boys had seen for variety and beauty. The Havasu River, foaming in torrents over Supai and Navajos Falls, fifty and seventy-five feet high, respectively, they found gliding through a narrow canyon for half a mile, in a valley matted with masses of trees, vines and ferns, the delicate green of whose foliage contrasted wonderfully with the dead gray walls of the deep, dark canyon at that point.

For some three miles below this the Pony Riders followed the smoothly-gliding stream through a canyon whose straight up and down walls of gray limestone seemed to meet overhead in the blue of the sky. Below they seemed to be in the tropics. During that first day in the Cataract they saw another wonder, that of the filmy clouds settling down and forming a roof over the Canyon. It was a marvelous sight before which the Pony Rider Boys were lost in wonder.

The Bridal Veil Falls they thought the most beautiful wonder of its kind they had ever seen. Here they saw the crystal waters dashing in clouds of spray through masses of ferns, moss and trees, one hundred and seventy-five feet perpendicularly into a seething pool below.

Their delight was in the innumerable caves found along the Canyon. In these were to be seen flowers fashioned out of the limestone, possessing wonderful colors, scintillating in the light of the torches, reds that glowed like points of fire, stalactites that glistened like the long, pointed icicles they had seen hanging from the eaves of their homes in Chillicothe. They discovered lace-work in most delicate tints, masses and masses of coral and festoons of stone sponges in all the caves they visited. There were little caves leading from larger caves, caves within caves, caves below caves, a perfect riot of caves and labyrinths all filled with these marvelous specimens of limestone.

"I think I would be content to live here always," breathed Tad after they had finished their explorations of the caves and passed on into a perfect jungle of tropical growth on their way to Ko-ho-ni-no, the canyon home of the Havasupais.

"You'd never be lonesome here," smiled Nance.

"Why don't you live down here, then?" asked Ned.

"Perhaps I don't live so far from here, after all," rejoined the guide.

"Do they have ghosts in this canyon?" asked Chunky apprehensively.

"Full of them!"

"Br-r-r!" shivered the fat boy.

"A wonderful place for scientific research," mused the Professor.

"Why don't you stay in Bright Angel for a while and study ghosts?" suggested Stacy.

"I decline to be drawn into so trivial a discussion," answered Professor Zepplin severely.

"You wouldn't think it was trivial were you to see one of those things."

"Perhaps the Professor, too, has overloaded his stomach some time before going to bed," spoke up Tad Butler.

"You are mistaken, young man. I never make a glutton of myself," was the grim retort.

"Now will you be good, Tad Butler?" chuckled Walter Perkins.

"Yes, I have nothing more to say," answered Tad, with a hearty laugh.

"We are getting down on the level now," the guide informed them.

Halting suddenly, Nance pointed to an overhanging ledge about half a mile down the valley. The boys gazed, shading their eyes, wondering what Nance saw.

"I see," said Tad.

"Then you see more than do the rest of us," answered Ned. "What is it?"

"It looks to me like a man."

"You have good eyes," nodded Nance.

"Is it a -- a man?" questioned Chunky.

"Yes, it is an Indian lookout. He sees us and is trying to decide whether or not our mission is a friendly one."

"Indians! Wow!" howled Chunky.

"We are in their home now, so behave yourself," warned Nance.

The Havasu River, which the riders followed, extended right on through the village, below which were many scattering homes of the red men, but the majority of them lived in the village itself. Almost the entire length of the creek, both in the village and below, the river is bordered with cottonwood, mesquite and other green trees, that furnish shade for the quaint village nestling in the heart of the greatCanyon.

The boys followed the water course until finally they

were approached by half a dozen men -- indians -- who had come out to meet them.

Nance made a sign. The Indians halted, gazed, then started forward. In the advance was the Kohot or native chief.

"Hello, Tom," greeted the guide.

"How!" said the chief.

"Tom is a funny name for an Indian," observed Chunky.

"His name is Chick-a-pan-a-gi, meaning 'the bat'," answered Jim smilingly.

"He looks the part," muttered the fat boy.

"Tom, I've brought some friends of mine down to see you and your folks. Have you anything to eat?"

"Plenty eat."

"Good."

"Plenty meala, meula. Kuku. No ski," answered the chief, meaning that they were stocked with flour, sugar, but no bacon.

"I know that language," confided Stacy to Tad. "It's Hog Latin."

"Magi back-a-tai-a?" asked the chief.

"Higgety-piggety," muttered Chunky.

"He means, 'have we come from the place of the roaring sound?'" translated Nance.

"You bet we have. Several of them," spoke up Ned.

"Doesn't he speak English?" asked Walter.

"Yes, he will soon. He likes a confidential chat with me in his own language first. By 'the place of the roaring sound' he means the big Canyon. How is Jennie, Tom?"

"Chi-i-wa him good."

"That's fine. We'll be moving along now. We are tired and want to rest and make peace with Chick-a-pan-gi and his people," said Nance.

The Kohot bowed, waved a hand to his followers, who turned, marching stolidly back toward the village, followed by the chief, then by Nance and his party.

"This sounds to me as if it were going to be a chow-chow party," grinned Stacy.

"For goodness' sake, behave yourself. Don't stir those Indians up. They are friendly enough, but Indians are sensitive," advised Tad.

"So am I," replied Chunky.

"You may be sorry that you are if you are not careful. I shall be uneasy all the time for fear you'll put your foot in it," said Tad.

"Just keep your own house in order. Mine will take

care of itself. There's the village."

"Surely enough," answered Tad, gazing inquiringly toward the scattered shacks or ha-was, as the native houses were called. These consisted of posts set up with a slight slant toward the center, over which was laid in several layers the long grass of the canyon. Ordinarily a bright, hued Indian blanket covered the opening. A tall man could not stand upright in a Havasupai ha-wa. They were merely hovels, but they were all sufficient for these people, who lived most of their lives out in the open.

The street was full of gaunt, fierce-looking dogs that the boys first mistook for coyotes. The dogs, ill-fed, were surly, making friends with no one, making threatening movements toward the newcomers in several instances. One of them seized the leg of Chunky's trousers.

"Call your dog off, Chief Chickadee!" yelled the fat boy.

The Indian merely grunted, whereupon the fat boy laid a hand on the butt of his revolver. A hand gripped his arm at the same time. The hand was Tad Butler's.

"You little idiot, take your hand away from there or I'll put a head on you right here! The dog won't hurt you." Tad was angry.

"No, you've scared him off, now. Of course he won't bite me, but he would have done so if he hadn't caught sight of you."

"I must be good dog medicine then," replied Tad

grimly. "But, never mind," he added, with a smile, "just try to behave yourself for a change."

About that time Chief Tom was leading out his squaw by an ear.

"White man see Chi-i-wa," grinned the chief.

Chi-i-wa gave them a toothless smile. She was the most repulsive-looking object the boys ever had looked upon. Chi-i-wa's hair came down to the neck, where it had been barbered off square all the way around. This was different from her august husband's. His hair lay in straight strands on his shoulders, while a band of gaudy red cloth, the badge of his office, was twisted over The forehead, binding the straight, black locks at the back of the head.

The squaw wore baggy trousers bound at the bottom with leggings, while over her shoulder was draped a red and white Indian blanket that was good to look upon. The brilliant reds of the blankets all through the village lent a touch of color that was very pleasing to the eye.

The chief's son was then brought out to shake hands with the white men, while Chi-i-wa squatted down and appeared to lose all interest in life. Dogs and children were by this time gathered about in great numbers regarding the new comers with no little curiosity.

The chief's son was introduced to the boys by Nance as "Afraid Of His Face."

Stacy surveyed the straight-limbed but ugly faced young buck critically.

"I don't blame him," said the fat boy.

"Don't blame him for what?" snapped Nance.

"For being afraid of his face. So am I."

The boys snickered, but their faces suddenly sobered at a sharp glance from the piercing eyes of the Kohot.

"Mi-ki-u-la," said Afraid Of His Face, pointing to the much-soiled trousers of Stacy Brown.

"He likes your trousers, he says," grinned the guide.

"Well, he can't have them, though he certainly does need trousers," decided Stacy reflectively, studying the muscular, half-naked limbs of the young buck. "He couldn't very well appear in polite society in that rig, could he, Tad?"

"Not unless he were going in swimming," smiled Tad.

It was at this point that Tad Butler himself came near getting into difficulties. The chief's son, having been ordered in a series of explosive guttural sounds to do something, had started away when a yellow, wolfish looking cur got in way. Afraid Of His Face gave the dog a vicious kick, then as if acting upon second thought he grabbed up the snarling dog, and twisting its front legs over on its back, dropped the yelping animal, giving it another kick before it touched the ground.

Tad's face went fiery red. He could not stand idly and witness the abuse of an animal. The lad leaped forward and stood confronting the young buck with flaming face. Tad would have struck the Indian had Nance not been on the spot. With a powerful hand he thrust Tad behind him, saying something in the Indian language to Afraid Of His Face, which caused the buck to smile faintly and proceed on his mission.

"If you had struck him you never would have gotten out of here alive," whispered the guide. Stacy had been a witness to the proceeding. He smiled sarcastically when Tad came back to where the fat boy was standing.

"Folks who live in glass houses, should not shy rocks," observed the fat boy wisely.

By that time the squaws were setting out corn cakes, dried peaches and a heap of savory meat that was served on a bark platter. The meal was spread on a bright blanket regardless of the fact that grease from the meat was dripping over the beautiful piece of weaving. The boys thought it a pity to see so wonderful a piece of work ruined so uselessly, but they made no comment. Then all sat down, the Indians squatting on their haunches, while the white men seated themselves on the ground. There were neither knives nor forks. Fingers were good enough for the noble red man.

First, before beginning the meal, the Kohot lighted a great pipe and took a single puff. Then he passed it to Professor Zepplin, who, with a sheepish look at the Pony Rider Boys, also took a puff.

Stacy came next. The chief handed the pipe to the fat boy in person. Stacy's face flushed.

"Thank you, but I don't smoke," he said politely. The lines of the chief's face tightened. It was an insult to refuse to smoke the pipe of peace when offered by the Kohot.

CHAPTER XXI

CHUNKY GETS A TURKISH BATH

"Put it to your lips. You don't have to smoke it," whispered Dad. "It won't do to refuse."

Stacy placed the stem to his lips, then, to the amazement of his fellows, drew heavily twice, forcing the smoke right down into his lungs.

Stacy's face grew fiery red, his cheeks puffed out. Smoke seemed to be coming out all over him. Ned declared afterwards that Stacy must be porous, for the smoke came out of his pockets. Then all of a sudden the fat boy coughed violently, and tumbled over backwards, choking, strangling, howling, while the Professor hammered him between the shoulders with the flat of his hand.

"You little idiot, why did you draw any of the stuff in?" whispered Professor Zepplin.

"Da -- Da -- Dad to -- to -- told me to! Ackerchew! Oh, wow!"

More choking, more sneezing and more strangling. The Professor laid the boy on the grass a little distance from the table, where not a smile had appeared on a single face. The Indians were grave and solemn, the Pony Rider Boys likewise, although almost at the explosive point. The others had merely passed the Pipe of peace across their lips and handed it on to the next. In this manner it had gone around the circle.

Then all hands began dipping into the meat with their fingers. This was too much for the red-faced boy lying on the grass. He sat up, uttered a volley of sneezes then unsteadily made his way back to the blanket table and sat down in his place. The Indians paid no attention to him, though sly glances were cast in his direction by his companions. For once, Ned Rector was discreet enough not to make any remarks. He knew that any such would call forth unpleasant words from Stacy.

The fat boy helped himself liberally to the meat. He tasted of it gingerly at first, then went at it greedily.

"That is the finest beef I ever ate," he said enthusiastically.

"You shouldn't make remarks about the food," whispered Tad. "They may not like it."

"I hope they don't like it. There'll be all the more left for me."

"I don't mean the food, I mean your remarks about it."

"Oh!"

"How many persons are there in your tribe, chief?" asked the Professor politely.

The chief looked at Dad.

"Two hundred and fifty, Professor," the guide made answer for their host. "They are a fine lot of Indians, too."

"Including the squaws, two hundred and fifty?"

"Yes."

"Do they not sit down with us?" asked Professor Zepplin, glancing up at Chi-i-wa and some of her sisters, who were standing muffled in their blankets, despite the heat of the day, gazing listlessly at the diners.

"Certainly not in the presence of the white man or heads of other tribes," answered Jim.

"Say, what is this meat?" whispered Chunky again, helping himself to another slice.

"Don't you know what that is?" answered Ned Rector.

"No. If I did, I shouldn't have asked."

"Why, that's lion meat."

"Li -- li -- lion meat?" gasped the boy.

"Sure thing."

Stacy appeared to suffer a sudden loss of appetite. He grew pale about the lips, his head whirled dizzily. Whether it were from the pipe of peace or the meat, he never knew. He did know that he was a sick boy almost on the instant. With a moan he toppled over on his back.

"I'm going to die," moaned the fat boy. "Carry me off somewhere. I don't want to die here," he begged weakly.

They placed him under the shade of a tree but instead of getting better the boy got worse: The Professor was disturbed.

"Put pale-face boy in to-hol-woh," grunted the chief. "To-hol-woh!" he exclaimed sharply.

Three squaws ran to a low structure of branches that were stuck into the ground, bent in and secured at the middle until it resembled an Esquimo hut in shape. The frame made by the branches was uncovered, but the women quickly threw some brightly colored blankets over the frame, the boys watching the proceeding with keen interest. They then hauled some hot rocks from a fire near by, thrusting these under the blankets into the enclosure, after which a pail of water also was put inside.

"Put fat boy in," commanded the Kohot. "Take um clothes off."

Chunky demurred feebly at this. The Professor glanced at Dad inquiringly.
Dad nodded, grinning from ear to ear.

"It's a sort of Russo-Turkish bath. It'll do him good. Wouldn't mind one myself right now," said Nance.

"All right, boys, fix him up and get him in."

"Dress him down, you mean," chuckled Ned.

At a word from the chief the squaws stumped listlessly to their ha-was and were seen no more for some time. About this time the Medicine man, a tall, angular, eagle-eyed Havasu, appeared on the scene, examining the to-hol-woh critically.

"What shall we do with him now?" called Tad, after they had stripped off all of Chunky's clothes except his underwear.

"Chuck him in," ordered the guide.

The Pony Rider Boys were filled with unholy glee at the prospect. They picked up the limp form of their companion, Stacy being too sick to offer more than faint, feeble protests. They tumbled him into what Ned called "The Hole In The Wall."

By this time the hot stones in the enclosure had raised the temperature of the to-hol-woh considerably. Stacy did not realize how hot it was at first, but he was destined to learn more about it a few minutes later.

Now the Medicine Man began to chant weirdly, calling upon the Havasupai gods, Hoko-ma-ta and To-cho-pa, which translated by the guide was:

"Let the heat come and enter within us, reach head, face and lungs, Go deep down in stomach, through arms, body, thighs. Thus shall we be purified, made well from all ill, Thus shall we be strengthened to keep back all that can harm, For heat alone gives life and force."

"Let heat enter our heads, Let heat enter our eyes, Let heat enter our ears, Let heat enter our nostrils -- "

Up to this time no sounds had come from the interior of the to-hol-woh. But now the fat boy half rolled out, gasping for breath. Ned, having picked up a paddle that lay near this impromptu Turkish bath, administered a resounding slap on Stacy's anatomy, while Tad and Walter threw him back roughly into the to-hol-woh.

Chunky moaned dismally.

"I'm being burned alive," he groaned. "They're torturing me to death."

"Let heat enter the feet, Let heat enter the knees, Let heat enter the legs -- "

"Lemme out of here!" yelled the sick boy, thrusting a tousled head through between the blankets covering the opening.

They pushed him back.

"It's the paddle for yours, and hard, if you come out before we tell you," cried Ned.

"Stay in as long as you can, Stacy. I am satisfied the treatment will benefit you," advised the Professor.

"I'm cooking," wailed Chunky.

"That's what you need. You've been underdone all your life," jeered Rector.

Throughout all of this the Havasus had sat about apparently taking no particular interest in the performance. They had all seen it before so many, many times. But Jim Nance's sides were shaking with laughter, and the Pony Rider Boys were dancing about in high glee. They did not get such a chance at Stacy Brown every day in the year, and were not going to miss a single second of this sort of fun.

"A brave lion tamer ought not to be afraid of a little heat," suggested Walt.

"That's so," agreed Ned.

"For heat alone gives life and force," crooned the Medicine Man.

He repeated the words of his chant twice over, naming pretty much every member in the body. It was a long process, but no one save Stacy Brown himself wearied of it.

At the conclusion of the second round of the chant, the Medicine Man, stooping over, sprinkled water upon the hot stones, reaching in under the blankets to do so.

Instantly the to-hol-woh was filled with a cloud of fierce, biting steam, that made each breath seem a breath of fire.

The Pony Rider Boys, understanding what this meant to the boy inside, unable to restrain themselves longer, gave vent to ear-splitting shouts of glee. Even the Indians turned to gaze at them in mild surprise.

"Take me out! I'm on fire!" yelled the fat boy lustily.

The Medicine Man thrust half a dozen other hot stones in, then sprinkled more water upon them.

"There's one more steaming for Chunky," sang Tad.

"There's one more roast for him," chanted Ned.

"We'll roast him till he's done," added Walter.

The Medicine Man sprinkled on more water.

"Ow, wow! Yeow, wow-wow!"

Anguished howls burst from the interior of the to-hol-woh. Then something else burst. The peak of the bath house seemed to rise right into the air. The sides burst out, flinging the blankets in all directions. Then a red-faced boy leaped out, and with a yell, fled on hot feet to the silvery Havasu River, where he plunged into a deep pool, the water choking down his howls of rage and pain.

The fat boy's Russo-Turkish bath had succeeded beyond the fondest expectations of his torturers.

CHAPTER XXII

A MAGICAL CURE

Pandemonium reigned in the Havasu village for a few minutes. The Medicine Man had been bowled over in Stacy's projectile-like flight. The Medicine Man leaped to his feet, eyes flashing. Some one pointed toward the creek. The Medicine Man leaped for the river.

Dad spoke sharply to the chief, whereupon the latter fired a volley of gutturals at the fleeing Medicine Man, who stopped so suddenly that he nearly lost his balance.

"Is the water deep in there?" cried the Professor.

"About ten feet," answered the guide.

"He'll drown!"

"No he won't drown, Professor," called Tad. "Chunky can swim like a fish. There he is now."

A head popped up from the water, followed by a face almost as red as the sandstone rocks on the great cliffs glowing off there in the afternoon sun.

"Oh, wow!" bellowed Stacy chokingly, as the waters

swallowed him up again. He came up once more and struck out for the bank, up which he struggled, then began racing up and down the edge of the stream yelling:

"I'm skinned alive! I'm flayed, disfigured! I'm par-boiled! Pour a bottle of oil over me. I tell you I'm --- "

"You're all right. Stop it!" commanded Tad sharply.

"Sprinkle me with flour the way mother used to do."

Tad walked over and laid a firm hand on the arm of the fat boy.

"You go back there and wipe off, then put on your clothes, or I'll skin you in earnest. I wouldn't be surprised if they'd scalp you if you continue to carry on in this way."

"Sea -- scalp me?" stammered Stacy.

"Yes. You surely have done enough to them to make them want to. Did you know you knocked over the Medicine Man?"

"Did I?"

"You did."

Stacy grinned.

"I'm glad of it. But that isn't a circumstance to what I'd like, to do to him if I could do it and get away with it.

"Well, how does it feel to be roasted?" questioned the

grinning Ned Rector, approaching them at this juncture.

"Who put up this job on me?" demanded Stacy angrily.

"Job? Why, it wasn't a job. You were a very sick man. Your case demanded instant treatment -- "

"Say, what was that meat we had for dinner, Tad?" asked Chunky suddenly.

"Deer meat."

"Oh, fiddle! Ned said it was cat meat and I -- I got sick. I'll get even with him for that."

"How do you feel?" asked the smiling Professor, coming up and slapping the fat boy on the shoulder.

"I -- I guess I'm well, but I don't believe I'll be able to sit down or lie down all the rest of the summer. No, don't ask me to put on my clothes. I can't wear them. My skin's all grown fast to my underwear. I'll have to wear these underclothes the rest of the season if I don't want to lose my skin. Oh, I'm in an awful fix."

"But you're well, so what's the odds?" laughed Tad.

"It does brace a fellow up to have that -- that -- what do you call it?"

"Hole In The Wall bath," nodded Ned.

"That's just the trouble. There wasn't any hole in the wall to let the heat out. Oh, it was awful. If you don't think it was, then some of you fellows get in there for a roast. Oh, I'm sore!"

Stacy limped off by himself, then stood leaning against a rock, still in his underwear, gazing moodily at the waters of Havasu River. Stacy was much chastened for the time being.

All at once the lad started. Ned Rector had laid a hand on his shoulder.

"Oh, it's you?"

"Yes. You aren't angry with me, are you, Chunky?"

"Angry with you?"

"Yes."

"Did you ever have a sore lip, Ned?"

"Of course I have," laughed Rector.

"When you couldn't have laughed at the funniest story you ever heard?"

"I guess that about describes it."

"Well, I've got a sore lip all over my body. If I were to be cross with you I'd crack the one big, sore lip and then you'd hear me yell," answered the fat boy solemnly. "No, I'm not angry with you, Ned."

Rector laughed softly.

"I don't want you to be. I'm always having a lot of fun with you and I expect to have a lot more, for you are the biggest little idiot I ever saw in my life."

"Yes, I am," agreed Stacy thoughtfully. "But how can you blame me, with the company I keep?"

"I've got nothing more to say, except that if you'll come back to what's his name's camp I'll help you put on your clothes. Come along. Don't miss all the fun."

Stacy decided that he would. By the time he had gotten on his clothes he felt better. He wandered off to another part of the village, where his attention was drawn to a game going on between a lot of native children who had squatted down on the ground.

Stacy asked what the game was. They told him it was "Hui-ta-qui-chi-ka," which he translated into "Have-a-chicken."

Most of these children were pupils at a school established by the United States government in the Canyon, and could speak a little English. Chunky entered into conversation with them at once, asking the names of each, but he never remembered the name of any of them afterwards. There was little Pu-ut, a demure faced savage with a string of glass beads around her neck; Somaja, round and plump, because of which she got her name, which, translated meant "watermelon." Then there was Vesna and many other names not so easy. Chunky decided that he would like to play "Have-a-chicken," too. The little savages were willing, so he took a seat in the semicircle with them.

Before the semicircle was a circle of small stones, with an opening at a certain point. This opening was called, Chunky learned, "Yam-si-kyalb-yi-ka," though the fat boy didn't attempt to pronounce it after his instructor. In the centre of the circle was another flat stone bearing the musical name of "Taa-bi-chi."

Sides were chosen and the game began. The first player begins by holding three pieces of short stick, black on one side, white on the other. These sticks are called "Toh-be-ya." The count depends upon the way the sticks fall. For instance, the following combinations will give an idea as to how the game is counted:

Three white sides up, 10; three blacks, 5; two blacks and a white up, 3; two whites and a black up, 2, and so on in many different combinations.

The reader may think this a tame sort of game, but Chunky didn't find it so. It grew so exciting that the fat boy found himself howling louder than any of the savages with whom he was playing. He was as much a savage as any of them, some of whom were of his own age. Every time he made a large point, Stacy would perform a war dance, howling, "Have-a-chicken! Have-a-chicken!"

The chief's son, who also had come into the game without being invited, was playing next to Stacy. Stacy in one of these outbursts trod on the bare feet of the young buck.

Afraid Of His Face, adopting the methods of his white brethren, rose in his might and smote the fat boy with his fist. Now, the spot where the fist of Afraid Of His Face landed had been parboiled in the "Hole In The Wall." Stacy Brown howled lustily, then he sailed in, both fists working like windmills. The Indian youngsters set up a weird chorus of yells and war whoops, while all hands from the chief's ha-wa started on a run for the scene.

CHAPTER XXIII

STACY AS AN INDIAN FIGHTER

In the meantime there was a lively scrimmage going on near the "Have-a-chicken" circle. The stones of the circle had been kicked away, the younger savages forming a human ring about the combatants.

Afraid Of His Face was much the superior of the fat boy in physical strength, but he knew nothing of the tricks of the boxer. Therefore Stacy had played a tattoo on the face of the Indian before the latter woke up to the fact that he was getting the worst of it.

In an unguarded moment the young buck put a smashing blow right on Stacy's nose, now extremely sensitive from its near boiling in the "Hole In The Wall."

Not being fast enough in the get away, the young buck received on his own face some of the blood that spurted from Brown's nose.

"Ow-wow!" wailed Chunky, rendered desperate by the severe pain at this tender point. But his rage made him cooler. Chunky made a feint. As Afraid Of His Face dodged the feint Stacy bumped the young Indian's nose.

"Have another," offered Stacy dryly, as his left drove in a blow that sent the young Indian to his back on the turf. Frightened screams came from some of the young Indian girls, who gazed dismayed at the human whirlwind into which Stacy had been transformed.

"Ugh!" roared Afraid Of His Face, and reached his feet again. "Ugh! Boy heap die! Plenty soon!"

Again the combatants closed in. There was a rattling give-and-take.

"Here! Stop that!" ordered Professor Zepplin, striding forward. The chief and his Indians were coming up also. The chief caught at one of the Professor's waving arms and drew him back.

"Let um fight," grunted the chief. He next spoke a few guttural words of command to his own people, who fell back, giving the combatants plenty of room.

"Yes, let 'em have it out!" roared the boys. "Stacy never will learn to behave, but this ought to help."

Stacy, having it all his own way with his fists, now received a kick from the buck that nearly ended the fight.

"Wow! That's your style, is it?" groaned Chunky, then he ducked, came up and planted a smashing blow on the buck's jaw that sent the latter fairly crashing to earth.

That ended the fight. Afraid Of His Face made a few futile struggles to get to his feet, then lay back wearily. Chunky puffed out his chest and strutted back and forth a few times.

"Huh!" grunted Chick-a-pan-a-gi. "Fat boy heap brave warrior."

"You bet I am. But it's nothing. You ought to see me in a real fight."

"Hurrah for Chunky!" shouted Ned Rector. "Hip, hip, hurrah!"

Professor Zepplin now strode forward, laying a heavy hand on the fat boy's shoulder.

"Ouch!" groaned Chunky. "Don't do that Don't you know I haven't any skin on my body?"

"You don't deserve to have any. Be good enough to explain how this trouble arose?"

The chief was asking the same question of the other young savages in his own language and they were telling him in a series of guttural explosions.

"It was this way, I was playing the game with them when I stepped on Elephant Face's foot. He didn't like it. I guess he has corns on his feet as well as on his face. He punched me. I punched him back. Then the show began. We had a little argument, with the result that you already have observed," answered Stacy pompously.

"You needn't get so chesty about it," rebuked Ned.

"Chief," said the Professor, turning to Chick-a-pan-a-gi, "I don't know what to say. I am deeply humiliated that one of our party should engage in a fight with -- "

"I didn't engage in any fight," protested Stacy. "It wasn't a fight, it was just a little argument."

"Silence!" thundered the Professor.

"I trust you will overlook the action of this boy. He was very much excited and --- "

"Fat boy him not blame. Fat boy him much brave warrior," grunted the chief. "Afraid Of His Face he go ha-wa. Stay all day, all night. Him not brave warrior."

The chief accentuated his disgust by prodding his homely son with the toe of a moccasin. Afraid Of his Face got up painfully, felt gingerly of his damaged nose, and with a surly grunt limped off toward his own ha-wa, there to remain in disgrace until the following day.

"Fat boy come smoke pipe of peace," grunted the chief.

"No, thank you. No more pieces of pipe for mine. I've had one experience. That's enough for a life time," answered Stacy.

"Stacy, if I see any more such unseemly conduct I shall send you home in disgrace," rebuked the Professor as they walked back to the village.

"The boy wasn't to blame, Professor," interceded Dad. "The buck pitched into him first. He had to defend himself."

"No, don't be too hard on Chunky," begged Tad. "You must remember that he wasn't quite himself. First to be boiled alive, then set upon by an Indian, I should say, would be quite enough to set anyone off his balance."

The Professor nodded. Perhaps they were right, after all. So long as the chief was not angry, why should he be? The chief, in his unemotional way, seemed pleased with the result of the encounter. But Professor Zepplin, of course, could not countenance fighting. That was a certainty. With a stern admonition to Chunky never to engage in another row while out with the Pony Rider Boys, the Professor agreed to let the matter drop.

The day was well spent by that time, and the party was invited to pass the night in the village, which they decided to do. The chief gave the Professor a cordial invitation to share his ha-wa with him, but after a sniff at the opening of the hovel Professor Zepplin decided that he would much prefer to sleep outside on the ground. The others concluded that they would do the same. The odors coming from the ha-was of the tribe were not at all inviting.

After sitting about the camp fire all the evening, the Pony Rider Boys wrapped themselves in their blankets and lay down to sleep under the stars with the now gloomy walls of the Canyon towering above them, the murmur of the silvery Havasu in their ears.

CHAPTER XXIV

CONCLUSION

The night was a restful one to most of the party, except as they were aroused by the barking of the dogs at frequent intervals, perhaps scenting some prowling animal in search of food.

Chunky was awakened by Tad at an early hour. The fat boy uttered a familiar "Oh, wow!" when he sought to get up, then lay back groaning.

"Why, what's the matter?" demanded Butler.

"My skin's shrunk," moaned Stacy. "It fits me so tight I -- I can't move."

"His skin's shrunk," chorused the Pony Rider Boys. "His skin is a misfit."

"Take it back and demand a new suit if you don't like it," laughed Ned Rector.

"It isn't any laughing matter. I tell you it's shrunk," protested Stacy.

"All right, it will do you good. You'll know you've got a skin. Last night you said it was all roasted off from you."

"It was. This is the new skin, about a billionth of an inch thick, and oh-h-h-h," moaned the lad, struggling to his feet. "I wish you had my skin, Ned Rector. No, I don't, either I -- I wish yours were drawn as tightly as mine."

"Come on for a run and you will feel better" cried Tad, grasping the fat boy by an arm and racing him down to the river and back, accompanied by a series of howls from Stacy. But the limbering-up process was a success. Stacy felt better. He was able to do full justice to the breakfast that was served on the greasy blanket shortly afterwards. For breakfast the white men shared their bacon with the chief, which the Indian ate, grunting appreciatively.

Before leaving, the boys bought some of the finer specimens of the Indian blankets, which they got remarkably cheap. They decided to do up a bale of these and send them home to their folks when they reached a place where there was a railroad. At present they were a good many miles from a railway, with little prospect even of seeing one for a matter of several weeks.

After breakfast they bade good-bye to the chief. Chunky wanted to shake hands with Afraid Of His Face, but the chief would not permit his young buck to leave the ha-wa. Chi-i-wa, the chief's wife, bade them a grudging good-bye without so much as turning her head, after which the party rode away, Chunky uttering dismal groans because the saddle hurt him, for the fat boy was still very tender.

"I know what I'll do when I get home," he said.

"So do I," laughed Tad.

"Well, what'll I do, if you know so much about it?"

"Why, you will puff out your chest and strut up and down Main Street for the edification of the natives of Chillicothe," answered Tad.

"That's what he'll do, for sure," jeered Ned. "But we'll be on hand to take him down a peg or two. Don't you forget that, Chunky."

Joking and enjoying themselves to the fullest, these brown-faced, hardy young travelers continued on, making camp that night by the roaring river, reaching Camp Butler the following forenoon.

Chow, the half breed pack-train man, met them with a long face. The party saw at once that something was wrong.

"What's happened?" snapped Nance.

"The dogs."

"What about them? Speak up."

"Him dead," announced the half breed stolidly.

"Dead?" cried Dad and the boys in one voice.

"Him dead."

"What caused their death?"

The half breed shook his head. All he knew was that two mornings before he had come in for breakfast, and upon going out again found the dogs stretched out on the ground dead. That there was another mystery facing them the boys saw clearly. Nance examined the carcasses of the dead hounds. His face was dark with anger when he had finished.

"It's my opinion that those hounds were poisoned," he declared.

"Poisoned!" exclaimed the boys.

"Yes. There's some mysterious work being done around this camp. I'm going to find out who is at the bottom of it; then you'll hear something drop that will be louder than a boulder falling off the rim of the Grand Canyon."

"This is a most remarkable state of affairs." said the Professor. "Surely you do not suspect the man Chow?"

"No, I don't suspect him. It's someone else. I had a talk with Chief Tom. He told me some things that set me thinking."

"What was it?" asked Tad.

"I'm not going to say anything about it just now, but I am going to have this camp guarded after to-night. We'll see whether folks can come in here and play tag with us in this fashion without answering to Jim Nance."

"I'll bet the ghost has been here again," spoke up Stacy.

"Ghost nothing!" exploded Nance.

"That's what you said before, or words to that effect," answered the fat boy. "You found I was right, though. Yes, sir, there are spirits around these diggings. One of them carried away my gun."

"We will divide the night into watches after this. I am not going to be caught napping again," announced Nance.

That night the guide sat up all night. Nothing occurred to arouse his suspicion. Next day they went out lion hunting without dogs. Nance got a shot at a cat, but missed him. The next day the Professor killed a cub that was hiding in a juniper tree. It was his first kill and put the Professor in high good humor. He explained all about it that night as they sat around the camp fire. Then the boys made him tell the story over again.

Nance took the first watch that night, remaining on duty until three in the morning, when he called Tad. The latter was wide awake on the instant, the mark of a good woodsman. Taking his rifle, he strolled out near the mustangs, where he sat down on a rock. Tad was shivering in the chill morning air, but after a time he overcame that. He grew drowsy after a half hour of waiting with nothing doing.

All of a sudden the lad sat up wide awake. He knew that he had heard something. That something was a stealthy footstep. The night was graying by this time, so that objects might be made out dimly. Tad stood up, swinging his rifle into position for quick use. For some moments he heard nothing further, then out of the bushes crept a shadowy figure.

"Chunky's ghost," was the thought that flashed into the mind of the young sentry. "No, I declare, if it isn't an Indian!"

It was an Indian, but the light was too dim to make anything out of the intruder. The Indian was crouched low and as Tad observed was treading on his toes, choosing a place for each step with infinite care. The watcher now understood why no moccasin tracks had been found about the camp, for he had no doubt that this fellow was the one who was responsible for all the mysterious occurrences in camp up to that time.

The Pony Rider boy did not move. He wanted to see what the Indian was going to do. Step by step the red man drew near to the canvas covered storage place, where they kept their supplies, arms, ammunition and the like. Into this shack the Indian slipped. Tad edged closer.

"I wonder what he's after this time?" whispered the lad. Tad thrilled with the thought that it had been left for him to solve the mystery.

His question was answered when, a few moments later, the silent figure of the Indian appeared creeping from the opening. He had something in his hands.

"I actually believe the fellow is carrying away our extra rifles," muttered the boy.

That was precisely what the redskin was doing. After glancing cautiously about, he started away in the same careful manner. Tad could have shot the man, but he would not do it, instead, he raised the rifle.

"Halt!" commanded the Pony Rider boy sharply.

For one startled instant the Indian stood poised as if for a spring. Then he did spring. Still gripping the rifles, he leaped across the opening and started away on fleet feet. He was running straight toward where the ponies were tethered.

Tad fired a shot over the head of the fleeing man, then started in pursuit. The Indian slashed the tether of Buckey, Stacy Brown's mustang, and with a yell to startle the animal, leaped on its back and was off.

"That's a game two can play at," gritted the Pony Rider, freeing his own pony in the same way and springing to its back.

The shot and the yell had brought the camp out in a twinkling. No one knew what had occurred, but the quick ears of the guide catching the pounding hoofs of the running mustangs, he knew that Tad was chasing someone.

"Everybody stay here and watch the camp!" he roared, running for his own pinto, which he mounted in the same way as had the Indian and Tad Butler.

Tad, in getting on Silver Face, had fumbled and dropped his rifle. There was no time to stop to recover it if he expected to catch the fleeing Indian. Under ordinary circumstances the boy knew that Silver Face was considerably faster than Buckey. But pursuit was not so easy, though the Indian, for the present, could go in but one direction.

The spirited mustang on which Tad Butler was

mounted, appearing to understand what was expected of him, swept on with the speed of the wind. Small branches cut the face of the Pony Rider like knife-blades as he split through a clump of junipers, then tore ahead, fairly sailing over logs, boulders and other obstructions.

The Pony Rider boy uttered a series of earsplitting yells. His object was to guide Jim Nance, who, he felt sure, would be not far behind him. The yells brought the guide straight as an arrow. Tad could plainly hear the foot beats of Buckey as the two riders tore down the Canyon, each at the imminent risk of his life.

"If he has a loaded gun, I'm a goner," groaned the lad. "But the ones he stole are empty, thank goodness! There he goes!"

The Indian had made a turn to the left into a smaller canyon. By this time the light was getting stronger. Tad was able to make out his man with more distinctness. The boy urged his pony forward with short, sharp yelps. The Indian was doing the same, but Tad was gaining on him every second. Now the boy uttered a perfect volley of shouts, hoping that Nance would understand when he got to the junction of the smaller canyon, that both pursued and pursuer had gone that way.

Nance not only understood, but he could hear Tad's yells up the canyon upon arriving at the junction.

"Stop or I'll shoot!" cried the boy.

The Indian turned and looked back. Then he urged Buckey on faster.

That one act convinced Tad that the redskin had no loaded rifle, else he would have used it at that moment.

With a yell of triumph the boy touched the pony with the rowels of his spurs. Silver Face shot ahead like a projectile. He was a tough little pony, and besides, his mettle was up. Now Tad gained foot by foot. He was almost up to the Indian, yelling like an Indian himself.

The redskin tried dodging tactics, hoping that Tad would shoot past him. Tad did nothing of the sort. The boy was watching his man with keen but glowing eyes. The call of the wild was strong in Tad Butler at that moment.

Suddenly the boy drew alongside. Utterly regardless of the danger to himself, he did a most unexpected thing. Tad threw himself from his own racing pony, landing with crushing force on top of the Indian.

Of course the two men tumbled to the ground like a flash. Then followed a battle, the most desperate in which Tad ever had been engaged. The boy howled lustily and fought like a cornered mountain lion. Of course his strength was as nothing compared with that of the Indian. All Tad could hope to do would be to keep the Indian engaged until help arrived.

Help did arrive within two minutes; help in the shape of Jim Nance, who, with the thought of his slain hounds rankling in his mind, was little better than a savage for the time being.

"Here!" shouted Tad. "Take him -- hustle!"

Then young Butler drew back, for Nance, seeing things

red before his eyes, was hardly capable of knowing friend from foe.

Whack! bump! buff!

How those big fists descended!

For three or four seconds only did the redskin make any defense. Then he cowered, stolidly, taking a punishment that he could not prevent.

"Don't kill the poor scoundrel, Dad!" yelled Tad, dancing about the pair.

But still Nance continued to hammer the now unresisting Indian.

"Stop it, Dad -- stop it!" Tad called sternly.

Then, as nothing else promised to avail, Tad rushed once more into the fray.

Dad was weakening from his own enormous expenditure of strength.

"Don't go any farther, Dad," Tad coaxed, catching one of Nance's arm and holding on.

"I guess I have about given the fellow what he needed," admitted the guide, rising.

As he stood above the Indian, Dad saw that the man did not move.

"I hope you didn't kill him, Dad," Tad went on swiftly.

"Why?" asked Jim Nance curiously.

"I don't like killings," returned Tad briefly. He bent over the Indian, finding that the latter had been only knocked out.

"We'd better take the redskin back to camp, hadn't we?" queried Tad, and Jim silently helped. In camp, the Indian was bound hand and foot. The camp fire was lighted and Tad went to work to resuscitate the red man.

At last the camp's prisoner was revived.

"Now, let's ask him about the thieveries that have been going on," suggested Ned Rector.

"Humph!" grinned Dad. "If you think you can make an Indian talk when he has been caught red-handed, then you try it."

Not a word would the Indian say. He even refused to look at his questioners, but lay on the ground, stolidly indifferent.

"He's a prowling Navajo," explained Nance. "You may be sure this is the fellow, Brown's 'spirit,' behind all our troubles. He's the chap who stole Brown's rifle, who raided this camp, who set the lion free and who poisoned my dogs -- so they wouldn't give warning."

"But why should he want to turn the lion loose?" Tad wanted to know.

"Because the Navajo Indians hold the mountain lion as sacred. The Navajo believes that his ancestors' spirits have taken refuge in the bodies of the mountain lions."

"I believe there must be a strong strain of mountain lion in this fellow, by the way he fought me," grimaced Tad.

"What shall we do with this redskin?" Chunky asked. "Shall we give him a big thrashing, or make him run the gauntlet?"

"Neither, I guess," replied Jim Nance, who had cooled down. "The wisest thing will be for us to take him straight to the Indian Agency. Uncle Sam pays agents to take care of Indian problems."

It was late that afternoon when the boys and their poisoner arrived at the Agency.

"I'll talk to him," said the agent, after he had ordered that the Indian be taken to a room inside.

An hour later the agent came out.

"The Navajo confesses to all the things you charge against him," announced the government official. "I thought I could make him talk. The redskin justifies himself by saying that your party made an effort to kill Navajo ancestors at wholesale."

"Humph!" grunted Jim Nance.

"What happens to the Navajo?" Walter asked curiously.

"He'll be kept within bounds after this," replied the agent. "For a starter he will be locked up for three months. Some other Navajos were out, but we got them all back except this one. Going back into the Canyon?"

Indeed they were. Late that afternoon the Pony Rider Boys began their journey of one hundred miles to the lower end of the Canyon.

From that latter point they were to go on into still newer fields of exploration, in search of new thrills, and were far more certain than they realized at that time of experiencing other adventures that should put all past happenings in the shade.

For the time being, however, we have gone as far as possible with the lads. We shall next meet them in the following volume of this series, which is published under the title, "*The Pony Rider Boys With The Texas Rangers; Or, On the Trail of the Border Bandits.*"

A rare treat lies just ahead for the reader of this new narrative, in which acquaintance will also be made with one of the most famous bodies of police in all the world, the Texas Rangers.

Choose from Thousands of 1stWorldLibrary Classics By

Horace Walpole
Horatio Alger, Jr.
Howard Pyle
Howard R. Garis
Hugh Lofting
Hugh Walpole
Humphry Ward
Ian Maclaren
Israel Abrahams
J.G.Austin
J. Henri Fabre
J. M. Barrie
J. Macdonald Oxley
J. S. Knowles
J. Storer Clouston
Jack London
Jacob Abbott
James Allen
James Lane Allen
James Andrews
James Baldwin
James DeMille
James Joyce
James Oliver Curwood
James Oppenheim
James Otis
Jane Austen
Jens Peter Jacobsen
Jerome K. Jerome
John Burroughs
John F. Kennedy
John Gay
John Glasworthy
John Habberton
John Joy Bell
John Milton
John Philip Sousa
Jonathan Swift
Joseph Carey
Joseph Conrad
Joseph Jacobs
Julian Hawthrone
Julies Vernes
Justin Huntly McCarthy
Kakuzo Okakura
Kenneth Grahame
Kate Langley Bosher
L. A. Abbot
L. T. Meade
L. Frank Baum
Laura Lee Hope
Laurence Housman
Leo Tolstoy
Leonid Andreyev
Lewis Carroll
Lilian Bell
Lloyd Osbourne
Louis Tracy
Louisa May Alcott
Lucy Fitch Perkins
Lucy Maud Montgomery
Lydia Miller Middleton
Lyndon Orr
M. H. Adams
Margaret E. Sangster
Margaret Vandercook
Maria Edgeworth
Maria Thompson Daviess
Mariano Azuela
Marion Polk Angellotti
Mark Overton
Mark Twain
Mary Austin
Mary Cole
Mary Rowlandson
Mary Wollstonecraft
Shelley
Max Beerbohm
Myra Kelly
Nathaniel Hawthrone
O. F. Walton
Oscar Wilde
Owen Johnson
P.G.Wodehouse
Paul and Mable Thorn
Paul G. Tomlinson
Paul Severing
Peter B. Kyne
Plato
R. Derby Holmes
R. L. Stevenson
Rabindranath Tagore
Rahul Alvares
Ralph Waldo Emmerson
Rene Descartes
Rex E. Beach
Richard Harding Davis
Richard Jefferies
Robert Barr
Robert Frost
Robert Gordon Anderson
Robert L. Drake
Robert Lansing
Robert Michael Ballantyne
Robert W. Chambers
Rosa Nouchette Carey
Ross Kay
Rudyard Kipling
Samuel B. Allison
Samuel Hopkins Adams
Sarah Bernhardt
Selma Lagerlof
Sherwood Anderson
Sigmund Freud
Standish O'Grady
Stanley Weyman
Stella Benson
Stephen Crane
Stewart Edward White
Stijn Streuvels
Swami Abhedananda
Swami Parmananda
T. S. Ackland
The Princess Der Ling
Thomas A. Janvier
Thomas A Kempis
Thomas Anderton
Thomas Bailey Aldrich
Thomas Bulfinch
Thomas De Quincey
Thomas H. Huxley
Thomas Hardy
Thomas More
Thornton W. Burgess
U. S. Grant
Valentine Williams
Victor Appleton
Virginia Woolf
Walter Scott
Washington Irving
Wilbur Lawton
Wilkie Collins
Willa Cather
Willard F. Baker
William Makepeace
Thackeray
William W. Walter
Winston Churchill
Yei Theodora Ozaki
Young E. Allison
Zane Grey

www.ingramcontent.com/pod-product-compliance
Lightning Source LLC
LaVergne TN
LVHW090601110826
845146LV00001B/214

9781421804378